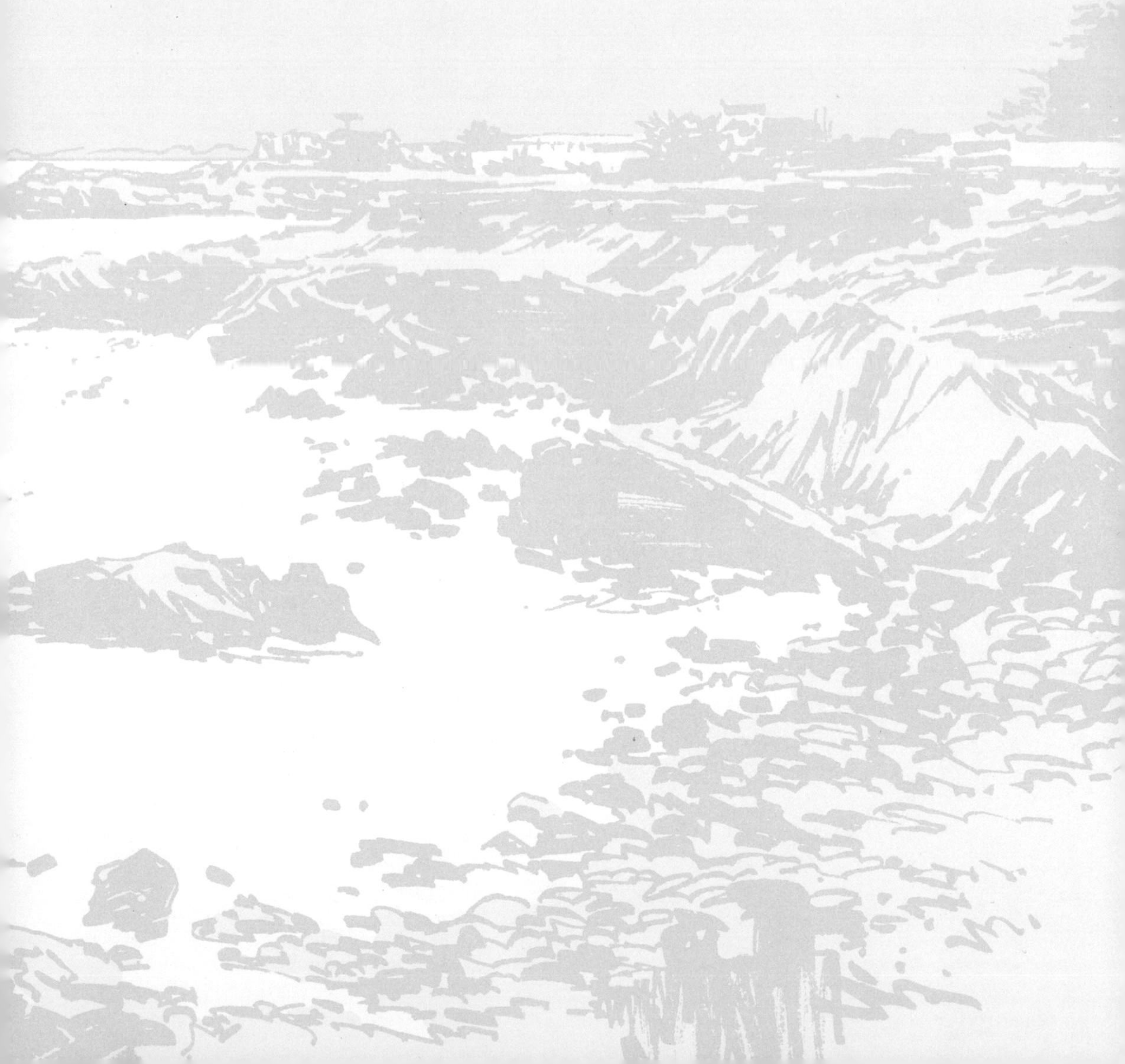

My Heroes Have Always Been Junkies

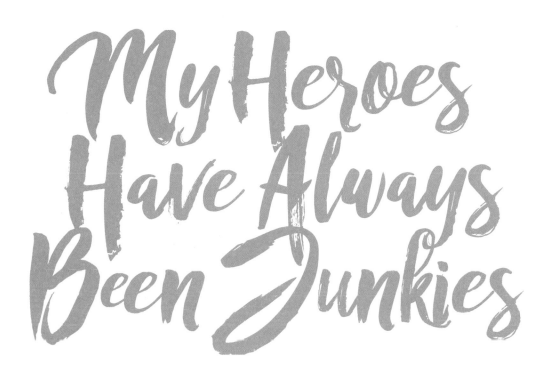

IMAGE COMICS, INC.

Robert Kirkman: Chief Operating Officer
Erik Larsen: Chief Financial Officer
Todd McFarlane: President
Marc Silvestri: Chief Executive Officer
Jim Valentino: Vice President
Eric Stephenson: Publisher / Chief Creative Officer
Corey Hart: Director of Sales
Jeff Boison: Director of Publishing Planning & Book Trade Sales
Chris Ross: Director of Digital Sales
Jeff Stang: Director of Specialty Sales
Kat Salazar: Director of PR & Marketing
Drew Gill: Art Director
Heather Doornink: Production Director
Nicole Lapalme: Controller

IMAGECOMICS.COM

My Heroes Have Always Been Junkies

a CRIMINAL novella by

Ed Brubaker
Sean Phillips

Colors by Jacob Phillips

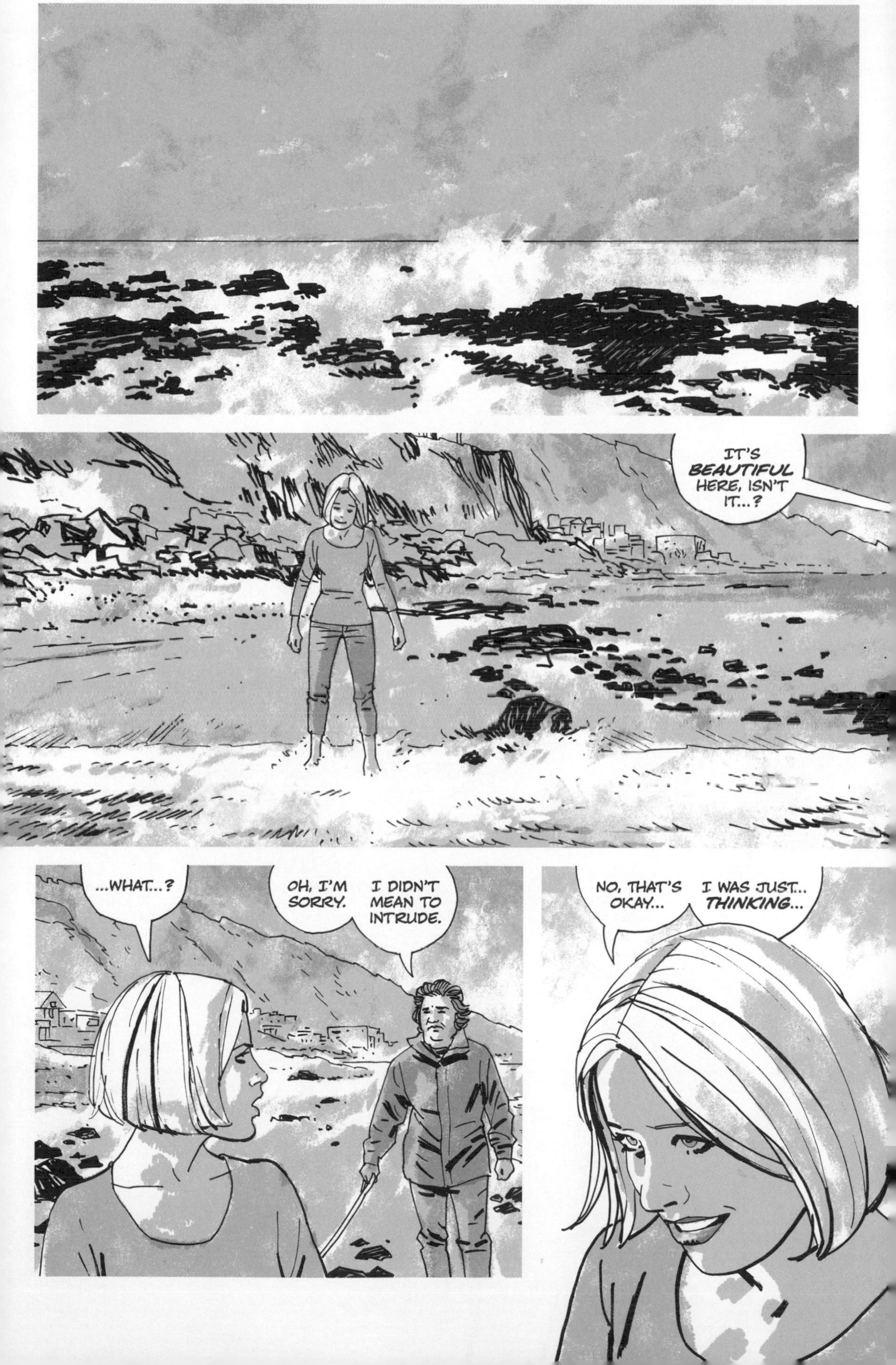
IT'S BEAUTIFUL HERE, ISN'T IT...?
...WHAT...?
OH, I'M SORRY.
I DIDN'T MEAN TO INTRUDE.
NO, THAT'S OKAY...
I WAS JUST... THINKING...

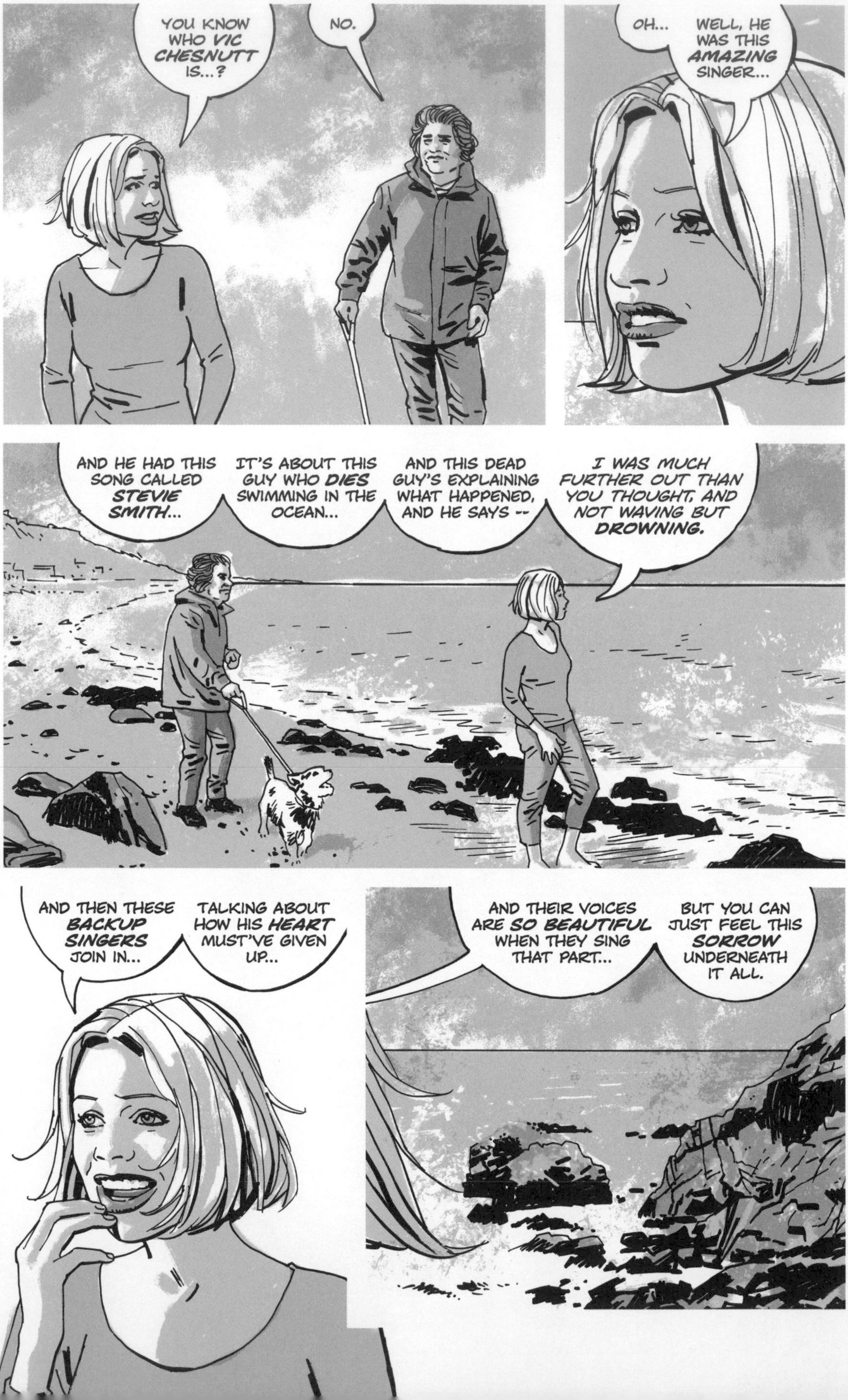
YOU KNOW WHO VIC CHESNUTT IS...?
NO.
OH...
WELL, HE WAS THIS AMAZING SINGER...
AND HE HAD THIS SONG CALLED STEVIE SMITH...
IT'S ABOUT THIS GUY WHO DIES SWIMMING IN THE OCEAN...
AND THIS DEAD GUY'S EXPLAINING WHAT HAPPENED, AND HE SAYS --
I WAS MUCH FURTHER OUT THAN YOU THOUGHT, AND NOT WAVING BUT DROWNING.
AND THEN THESE BACKUP SINGERS JOIN IN...
TALKING ABOUT HOW HIS HEART MUST'VE GIVEN UP...
AND THEIR VOICES ARE SO BEAUTIFUL WHEN THEY SING THAT PART...
BUT YOU CAN JUST FEEL THIS SORROW UNDERNEATH IT ALL.

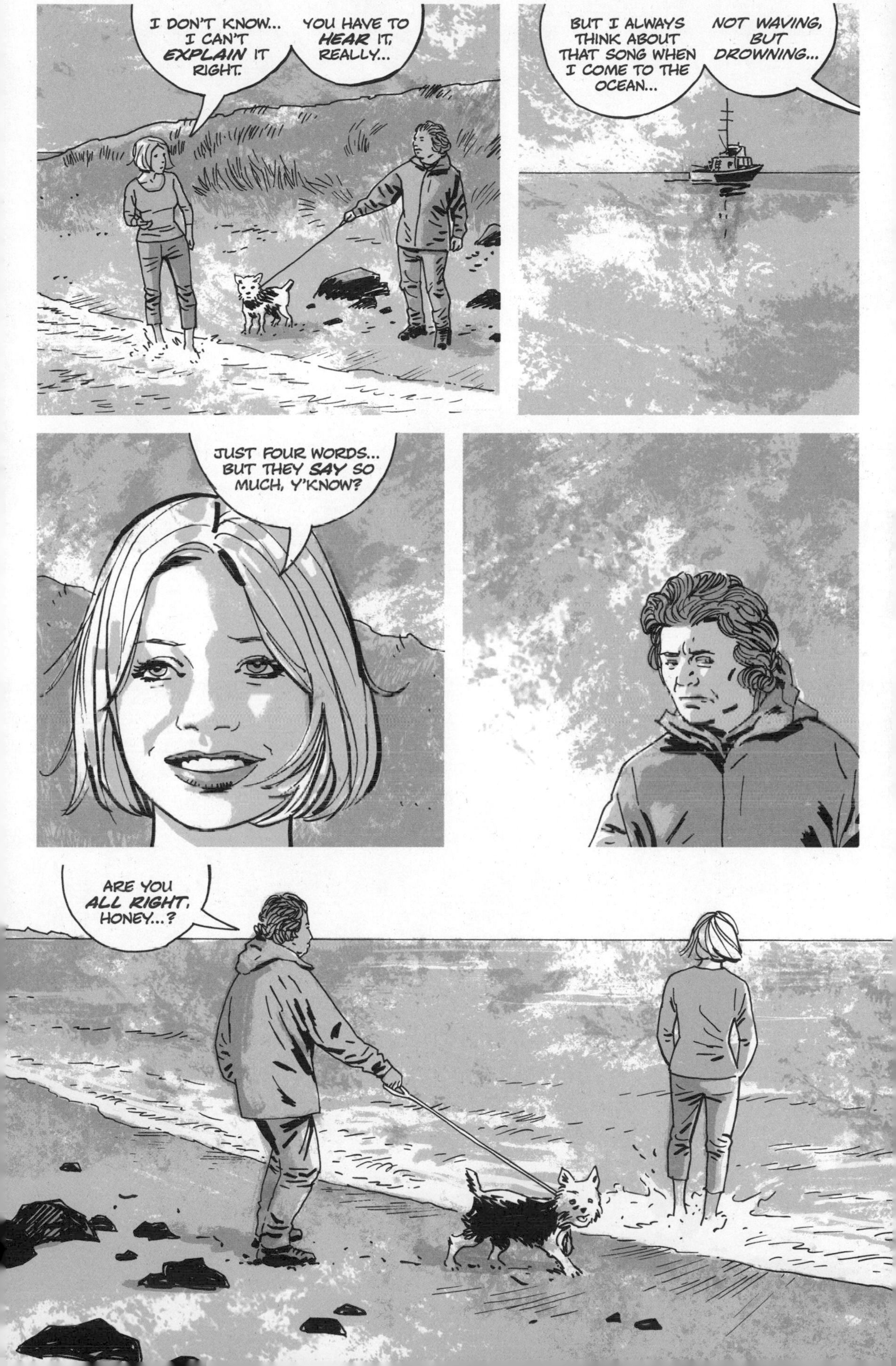
I DON'T KNOW... I CAN'T EXPLAIN IT RIGHT.
YOU HAVE TO HEAR IT, REALLY...
BUT I ALWAYS THINK ABOUT THAT SONG WHEN I COME TO THE OCEAN...
NOT WAVING, BUT DROWNING...
JUST FOUR WORDS... BUT THEY SAY SO MUCH, Y'KNOW?
ARE YOU ALL RIGHT, HONEY...?

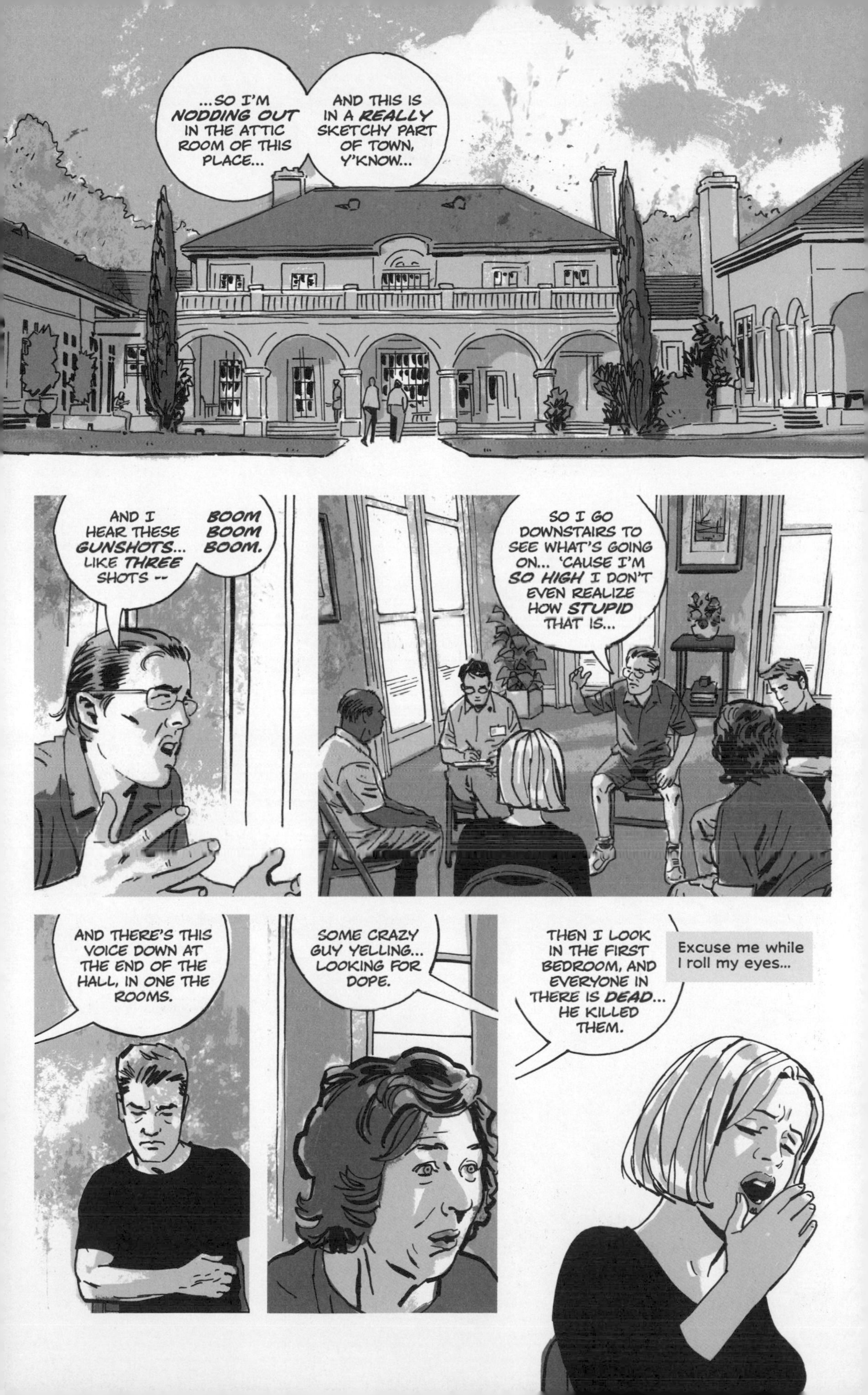
...SO I'M NODDING OUT IN THE ATTIC ROOM OF THIS PLACE...
AND THIS IS IN A REALLY SKETCHY PART OF TOWN, Y'KNOW...
AND I HEAR THESE GUNSHOTS... LIKE THREE SHOTS --
BOOM BOOM BOOM.
SO I GO DOWNSTAIRS TO SEE WHAT'S GOING ON... 'CAUSE I'M SO HIGH I DON'T EVEN REALIZE HOW STUPID THAT IS...
AND THERE'S THIS VOICE DOWN AT THE END OF THE HALL, IN ONE THE ROOMS.
SOME CRAZY GUY YELLING... LOOKING FOR DOPE.
THEN I LOOK IN THE FIRST BEDROOM, AND EVERYONE IN THERE IS DEAD... HE KILLED THEM.
Excuse me while I roll my eyes...

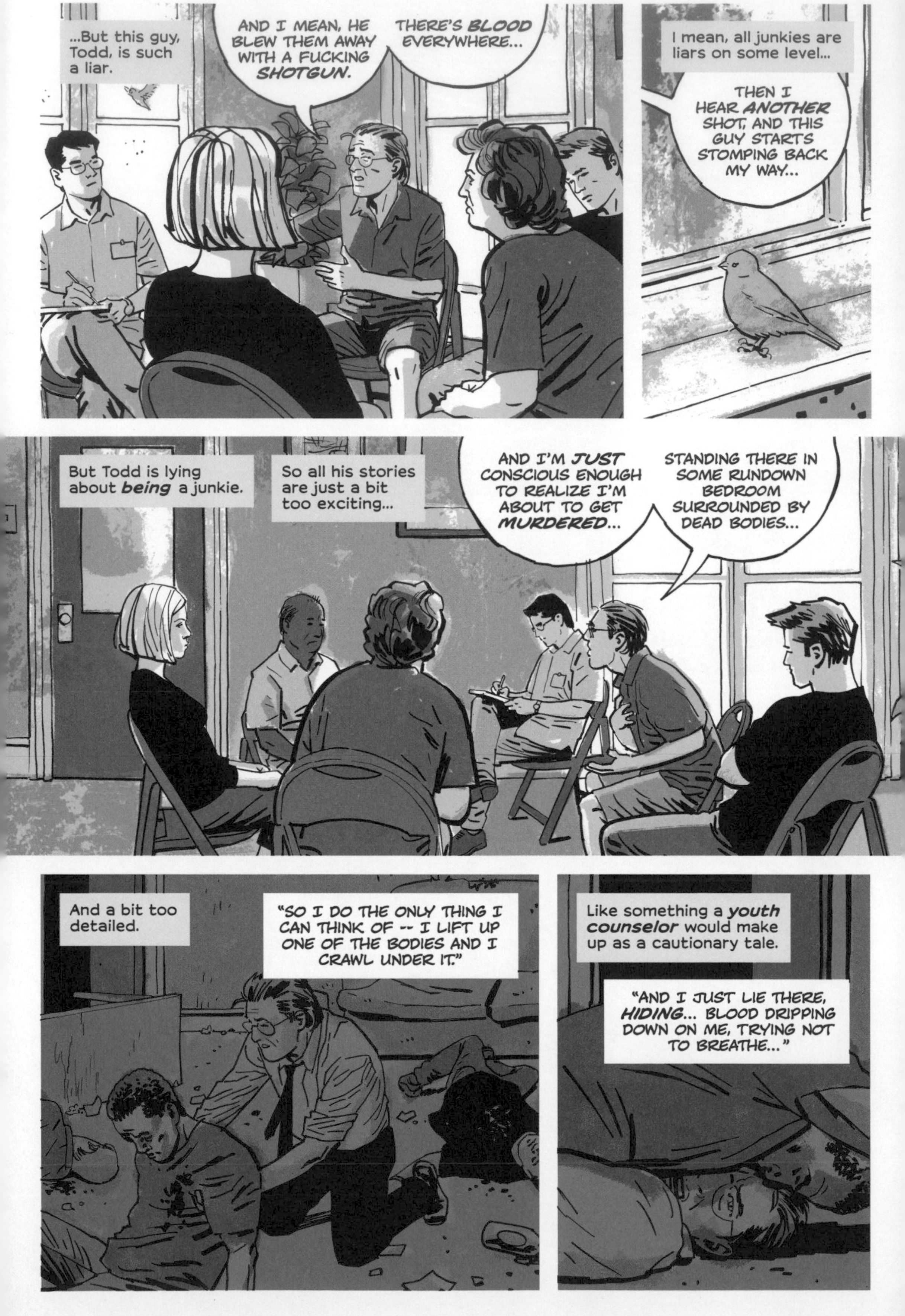
...But this guy, Todd, is such a liar.
AND I MEAN, HE BLEW THEM AWAY WITH A FUCKING SHOTGUN.
THERE'S BLOOD EVERYWHERE...
I mean, all junkies are liars on some level...
THEN I HEAR ANOTHER SHOT, AND THIS GUY STARTS STOMPING BACK MY WAY...
But Todd is lying about being a junkie.
So all his stories are just a bit too exciting...
AND I'M JUST CONSCIOUS ENOUGH TO REALIZE I'M ABOUT TO GET MURDERED...
STANDING THERE IN SOME RUNDOWN BEDROOM SURROUNDED BY DEAD BODIES...
And a bit too detailed.
"SO I DO THE ONLY THING I CAN THINK OF -- I LIFT UP ONE OF THE BODIES AND I CRAWL UNDER IT."
Like something a youth counselor would make up as a cautionary tale.
"AND I JUST LIE THERE, HIDING... BLOOD DRIPPING DOWN ON ME, TRYING NOT TO BREATHE..."

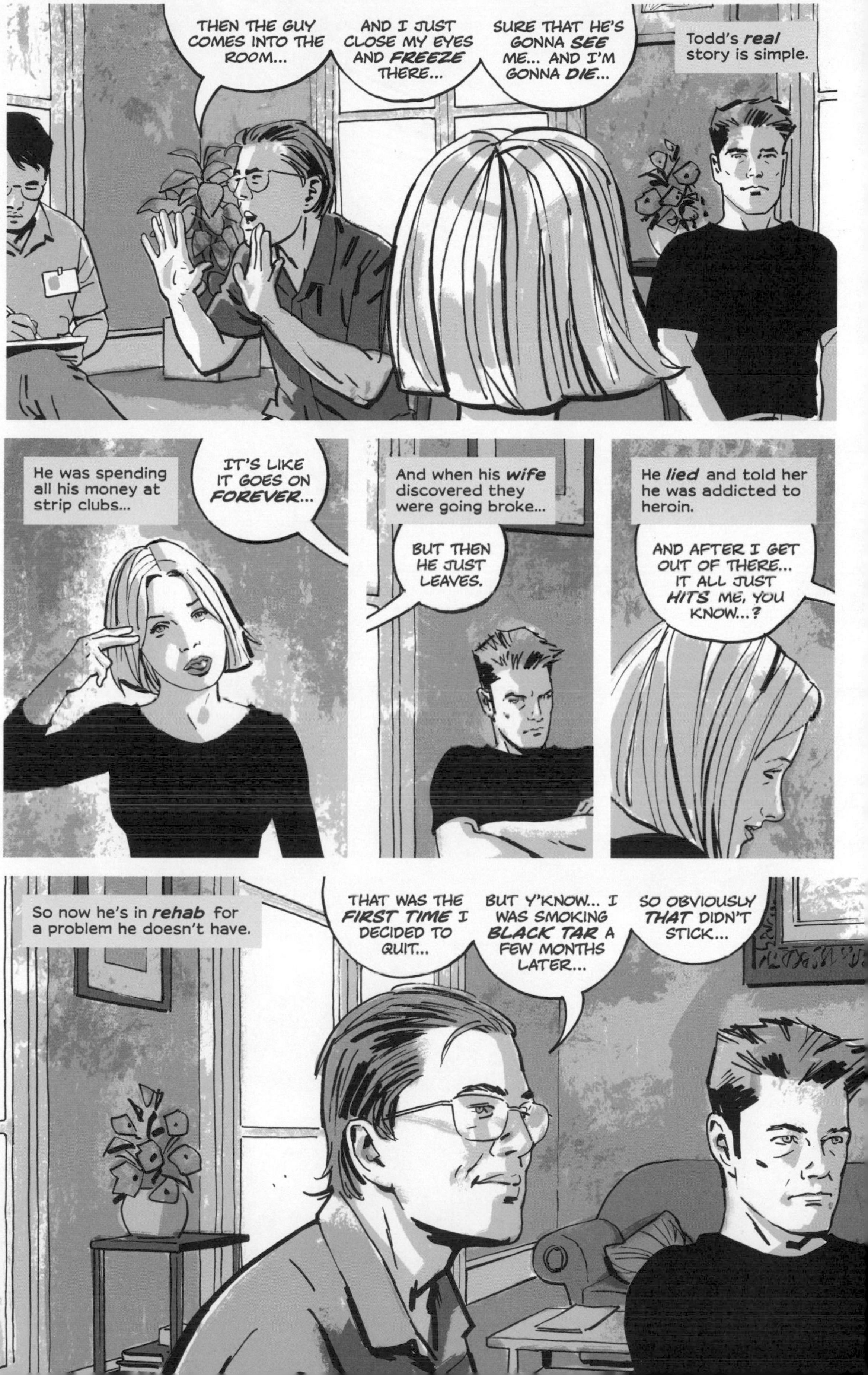
THEN THE GUY COMES INTO THE ROOM...
AND I JUST CLOSE MY EYES AND *FREEZE* THERE...
SURE THAT HE'S GONNA *SEE* ME... AND I'M GONNA *DIE*...
Todd's *real* story is simple.
He was spending all his money at strip clubs...
IT'S LIKE IT GOES ON *FOREVER*...
And when his *wife* discovered they were going broke...
BUT THEN HE JUST LEAVES.
He *lied* and told her he was addicted to heroin.
AND AFTER I GET OUT OF THERE... IT ALL JUST *HITS* ME, YOU KNOW...?
So now he's in *rehab* for a problem he doesn't have.
THAT WAS THE *FIRST TIME* I DECIDED TO QUIT...
BUT Y'KNOW... I WAS SMOKING *BLACK TAR* A FEW MONTHS LATER...
SO OBVIOUSLY *THAT* DIDN'T STICK...

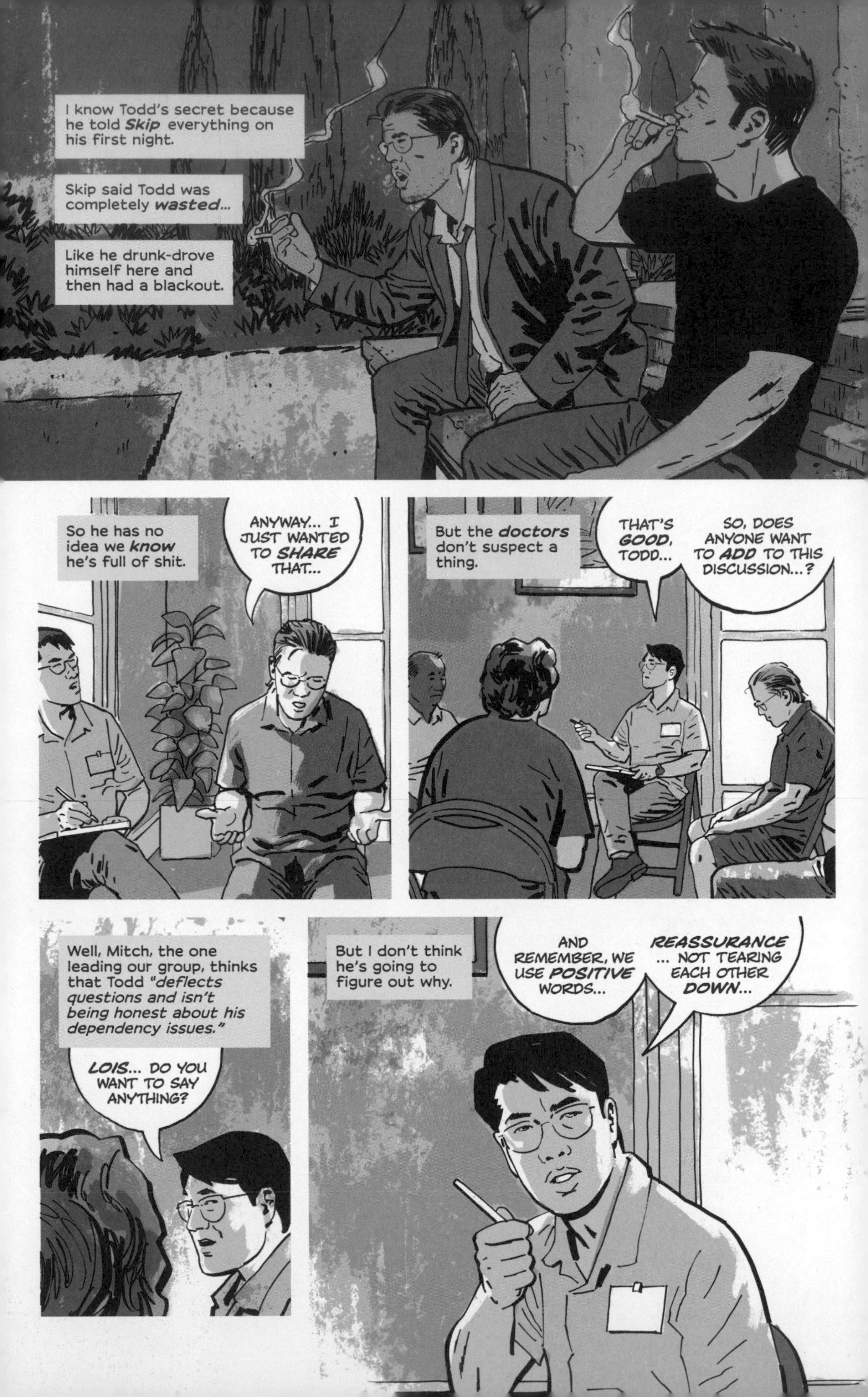
I know Todd's secret because he told *Skip* everything on his first night.
Skip said Todd was completely *wasted*...
Like he drunk-drove himself here and then had a blackout.
So he has no idea we *know* he's full of shit.
ANYWAY... I JUST WANTED TO *SHARE* THAT...
But the *doctors* don't suspect a thing.
THAT'S *GOOD*, TODD...
SO, DOES ANYONE WANT TO *ADD* TO THIS DISCUSSION...?
Well, Mitch, the one leading our group, thinks that Todd "*deflects questions and isn't being honest about his dependency issues.*"
LOIS... DO YOU WANT TO SAY ANYTHING?
But I don't think he's going to figure out why.
AND REMEMBER, WE USE *POSITIVE* WORDS...
REASSURANCE ... NOT TEARING EACH OTHER *DOWN*...

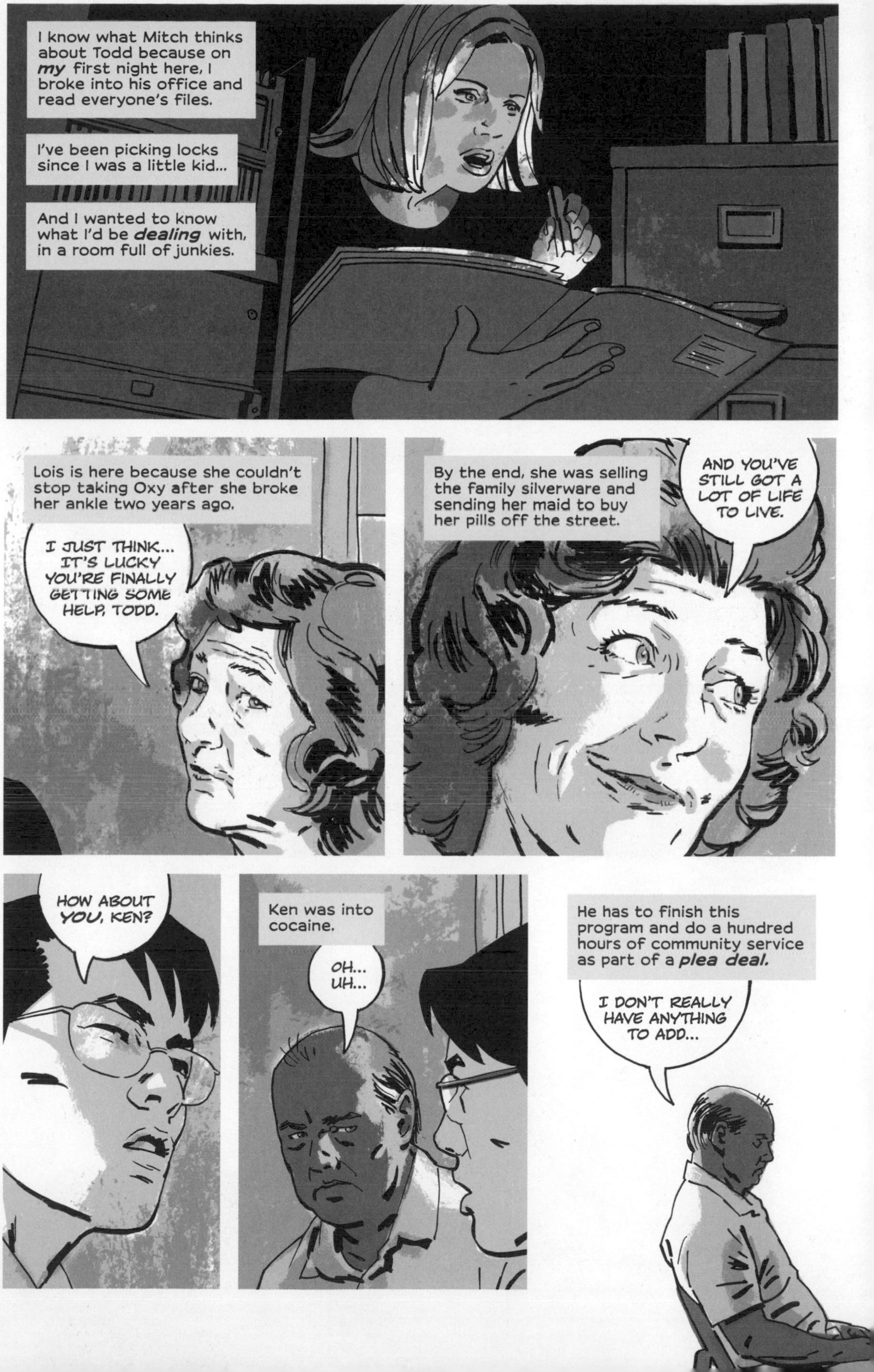
I know what Mitch thinks about Todd because on *my* first night here, I broke into his office and read everyone's files.
I've been picking locks since I was a little kid...
And I wanted to know what I'd be *dealing* with, in a room full of junkies.
Lois is here because she couldn't stop taking Oxy after she broke her ankle two years ago.
I JUST THINK... IT'S LUCKY YOU'RE FINALLY GETTING SOME HELP, TODD.
By the end, she was selling the family silverware and sending her maid to buy her pills off the street.
AND YOU'VE STILL GOT A LOT OF LIFE TO LIVE.
HOW ABOUT *YOU*, KEN?
Ken was into cocaine.
OH... UH...
He has to finish this program and do a hundred hours of community service as part of a *plea deal.*
I DON'T REALLY HAVE ANYTHING TO ADD...

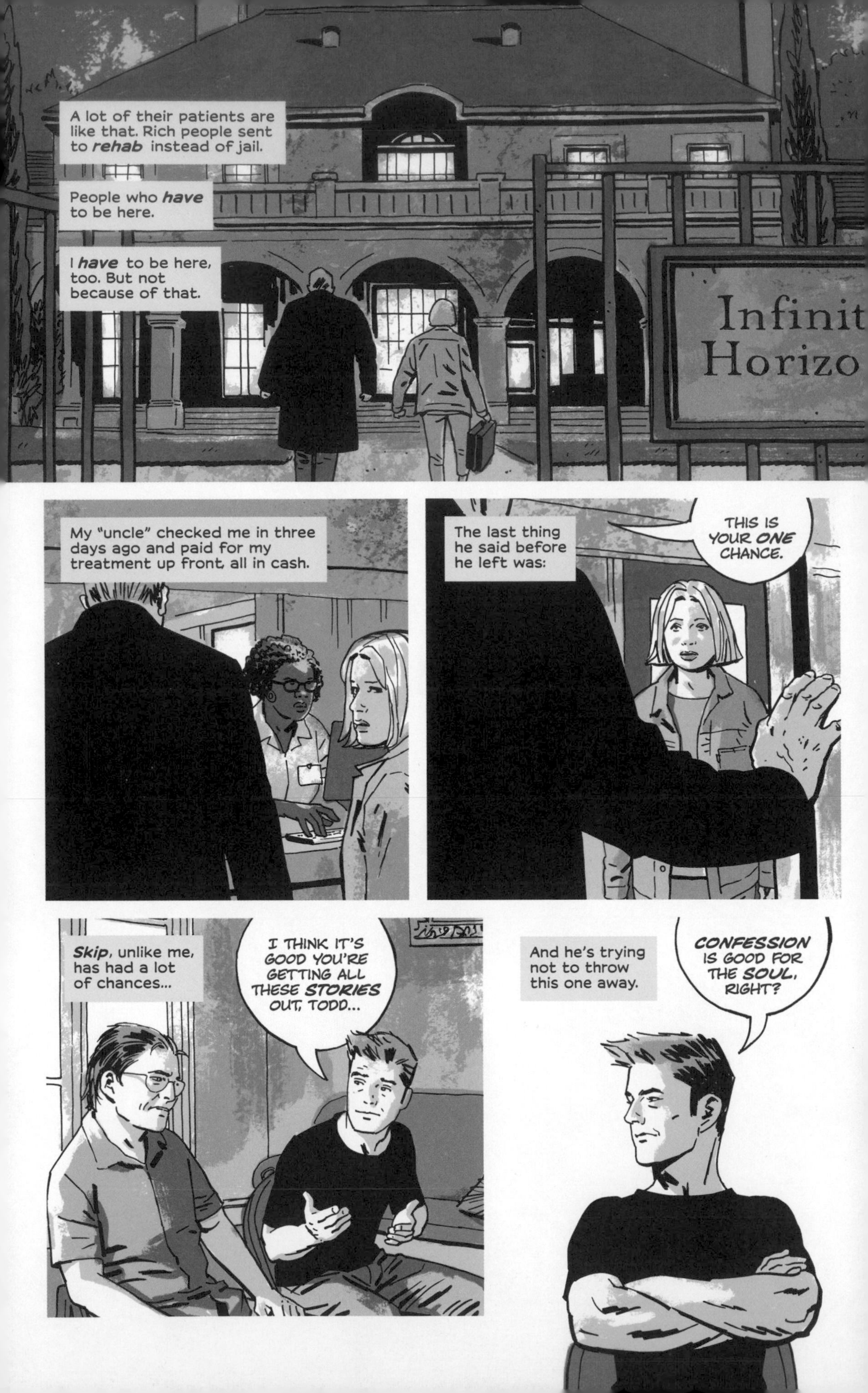
A lot of their patients are like that. Rich people sent to *rehab* instead of jail.
People who *have* to be here.
I *have* to be here, too. But not because of that.
Infinit
Horizo
My "uncle" checked me in three days ago and paid for my treatment up front, all in cash.
The last thing he said before he left was:
THIS IS YOUR *ONE* CHANCE.
Skip, unlike me, has had a lot of chances...
I THINK IT'S GOOD YOU'RE GETTING ALL THESE *STORIES* OUT, TODD...
And he's trying not to throw this one away.
CONFESSION IS GOOD FOR THE *SOUL*, RIGHT?

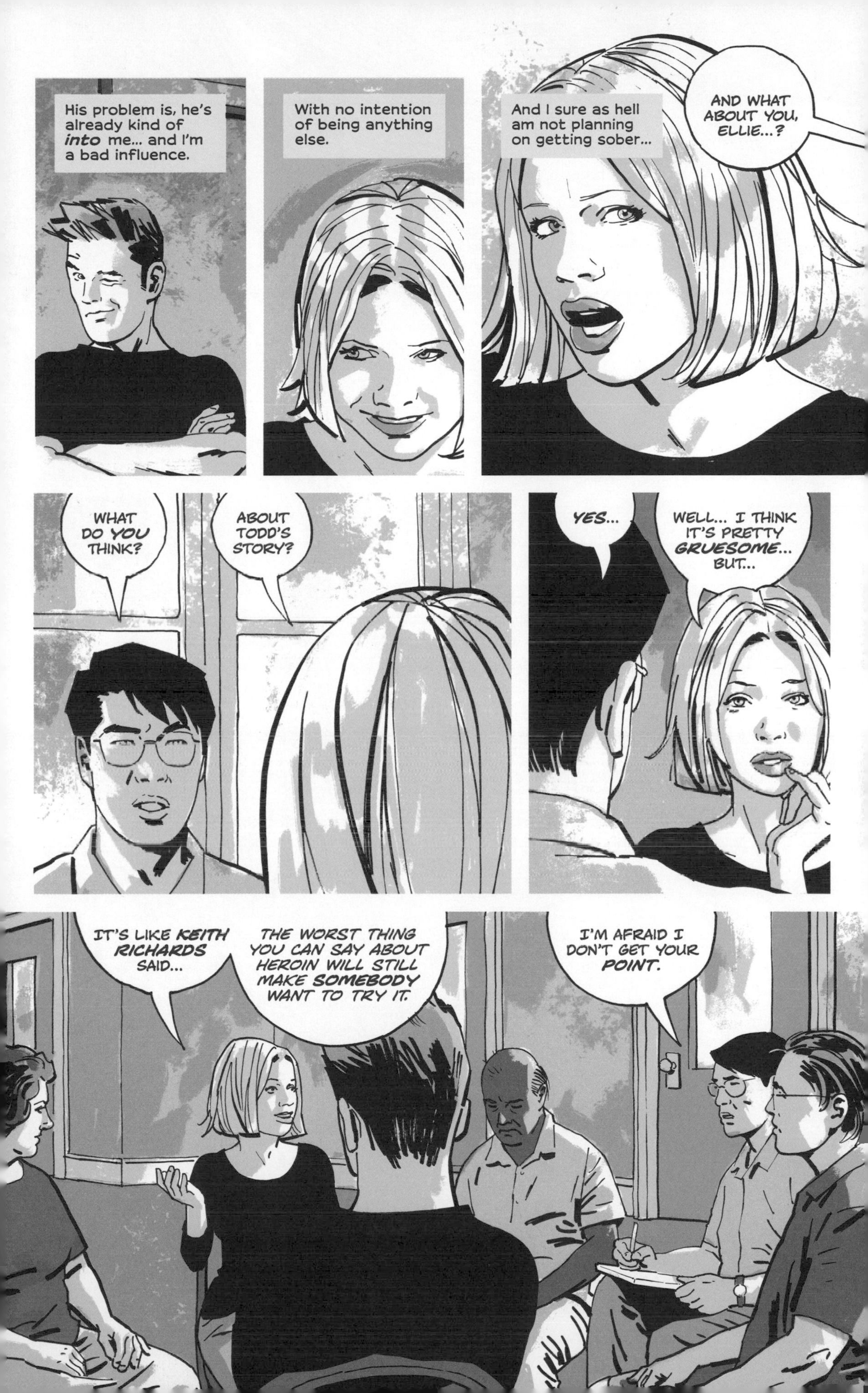

His problem is, he's already kind of *into* me... and I'm a bad influence.
With no intention of being anything else.
And I sure as hell am not planning on getting sober...
AND WHAT ABOUT YOU, ELLIE...?
WHAT DO *YOU* THINK?
ABOUT TODD'S STORY?
YES...
WELL... I THINK IT'S PRETTY *GRUESOME*... BUT...
IT'S LIKE *KEITH RICHARDS* SAID...
THE WORST THING YOU CAN SAY ABOUT HEROIN WILL STILL MAKE *SOMEBODY* WANT TO TRY IT.
I'M AFRAID I DON'T GET YOUR *POINT*.

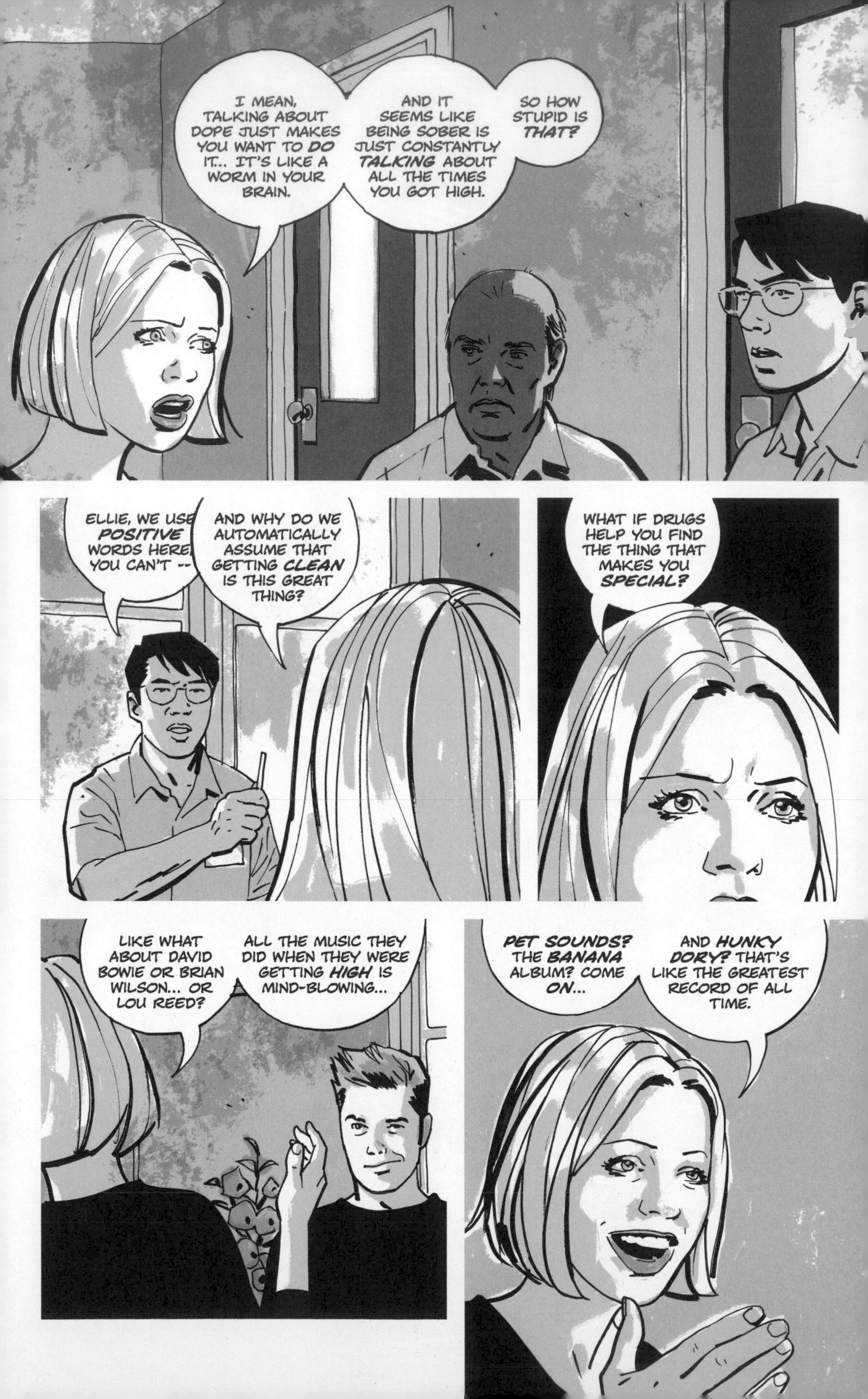
I MEAN, TALKING ABOUT DOPE JUST MAKES YOU WANT TO DO IT... IT'S LIKE A WORM IN YOUR BRAIN.
AND IT SEEMS LIKE BEING SOBER IS JUST CONSTANTLY TALKING ABOUT ALL THE TIMES YOU GOT HIGH.
SO HOW STUPID IS THAT?
ELLIE, WE USE POSITIVE WORDS HERE. YOU CAN'T --
AND WHY DO WE AUTOMATICALLY ASSUME THAT GETTING CLEAN IS THIS GREAT THING?
WHAT IF DRUGS HELP YOU FIND THE THING THAT MAKES YOU SPECIAL?
LIKE WHAT ABOUT DAVID BOWIE OR BRIAN WILSON... OR LOU REED?
ALL THE MUSIC THEY DID WHEN THEY WERE GETTING HIGH IS MIND-BLOWING...
PET SOUNDS? THE BANANA ALBUM? COME ON...
AND HUNKY DORY? THAT'S LIKE THE GREATEST RECORD OF ALL TIME.

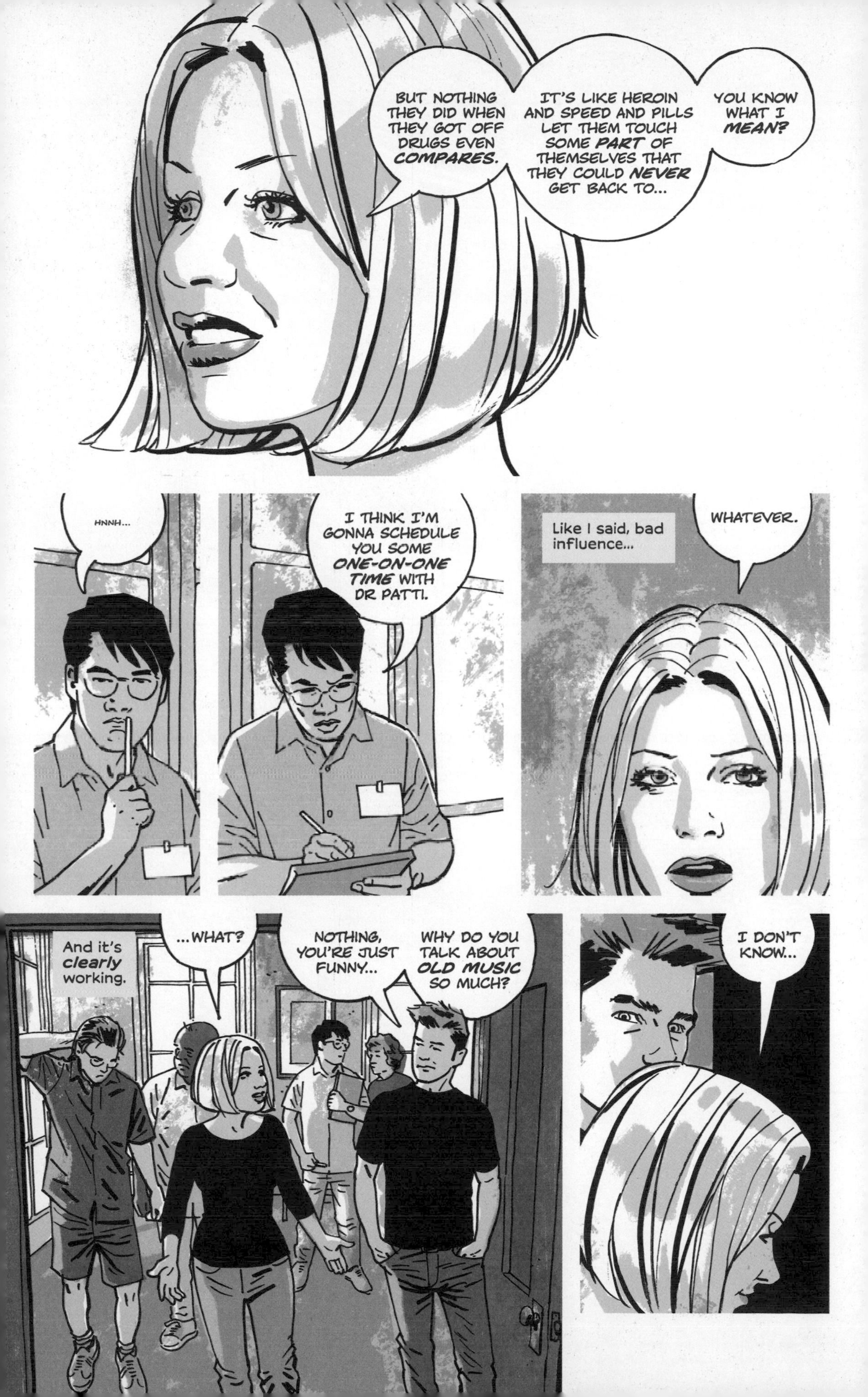
BUT NOTHING THEY DID WHEN THEY GOT OFF DRUGS EVEN COMPARES.
IT'S LIKE HEROIN AND SPEED AND PILLS LET THEM TOUCH SOME PART OF THEMSELVES THAT THEY COULD NEVER GET BACK TO...
YOU KNOW WHAT I MEAN?
HNNH...
I THINK I'M GONNA SCHEDULE YOU SOME ONE-ON-ONE TIME WITH DR PATTI.
Like I said, bad influence...
WHATEVER.
And it's clearly working.
...WHAT?
NOTHING, YOU'RE JUST FUNNY...
WHY DO YOU TALK ABOUT OLD MUSIC SO MUCH?
I DON'T KNOW...

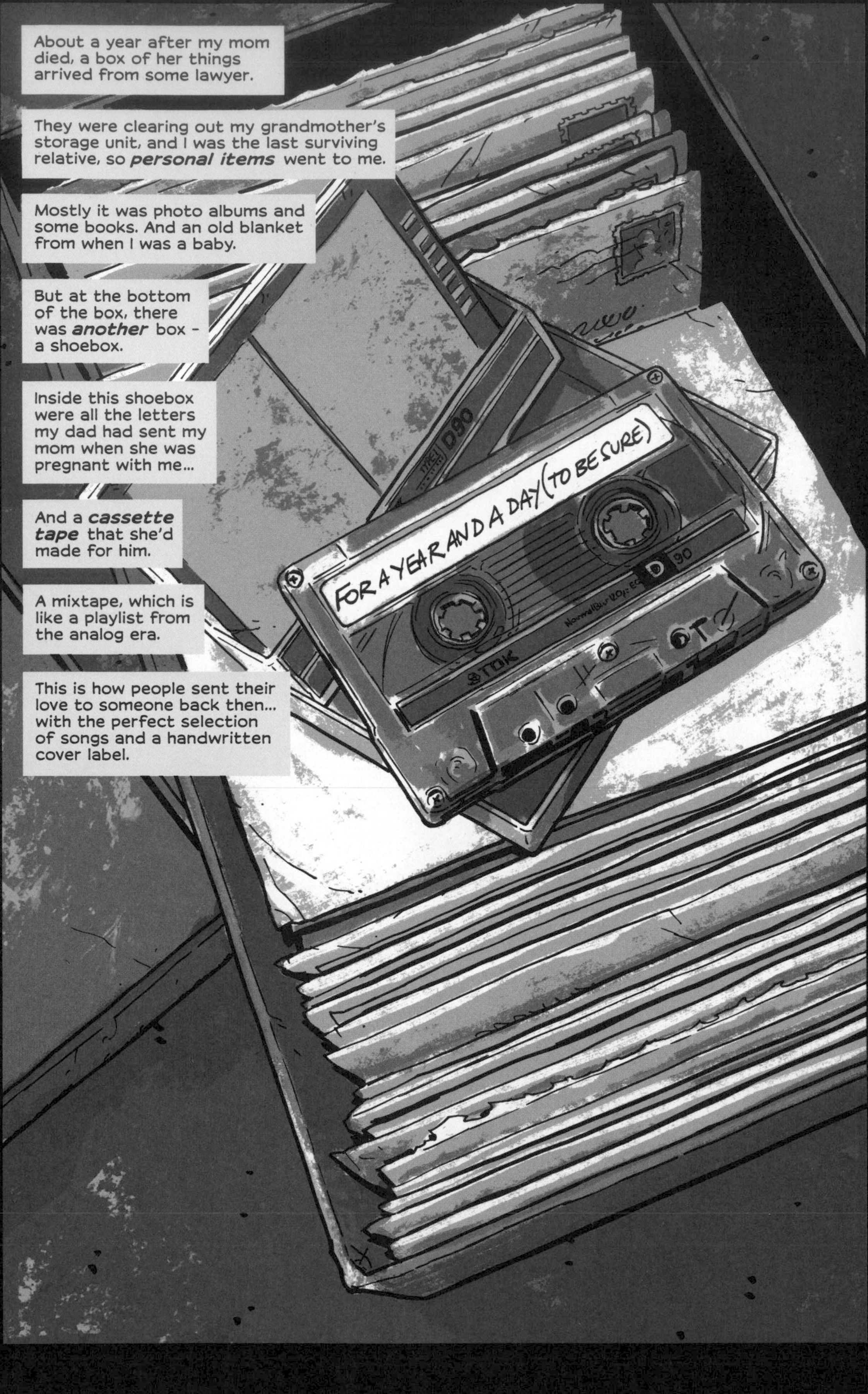
About a year after my mom died, a box of her things arrived from some lawyer.
They were clearing out my grandmother's storage unit, and I was the last surviving relative, so ***personal items*** went to me.
Mostly it was photo albums and some books. And an old blanket from when I was a baby.
But at the bottom of the box, there was ***another*** box - a shoebox.
Inside this shoebox were all the letters my dad had sent my mom when she was pregnant with me...
And a ***cassette tape*** that she'd made for him.
A mixtape, which is like a playlist from the analog era.
This is how people sent their love to someone back then... with the perfect selection of songs and a handwritten cover label.
FOR A YEAR AND A DAY (TO BE SURE)
TDK
D90

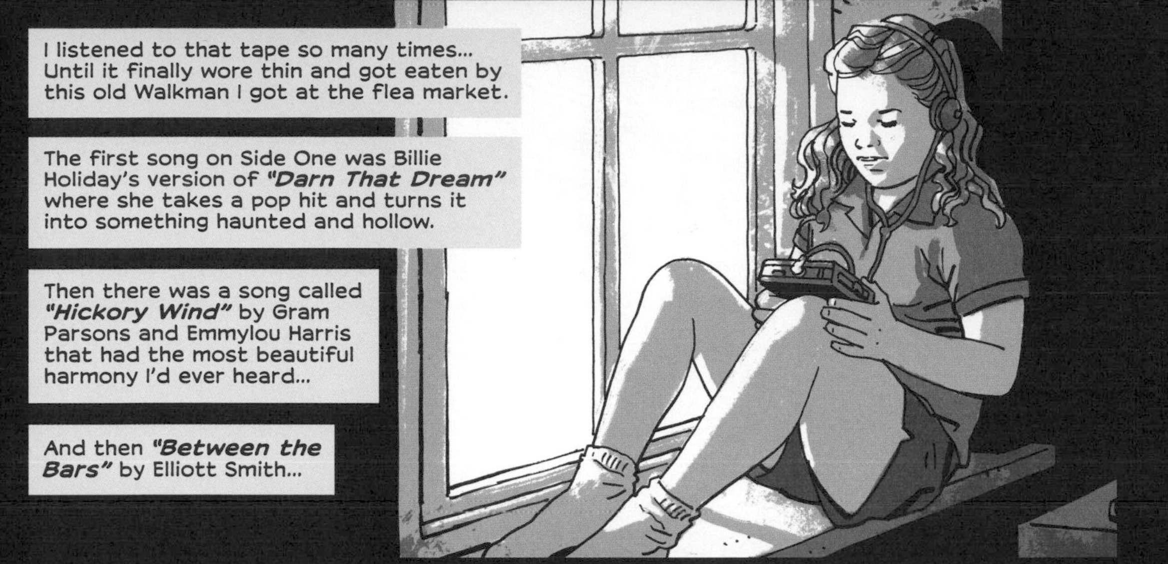
I listened to that tape so many times... Until it finally wore thin and got eaten by this old Walkman I got at the flea market.
The first song on Side One was Billie Holiday's version of *"Darn That Dream"* where she takes a pop hit and turns it into something haunted and hollow.
Then there was a song called *"Hickory Wind"* by Gram Parsons and Emmylou Harris that had the most beautiful harmony I'd ever heard...
And then *"Between the Bars"* by Elliott Smith...

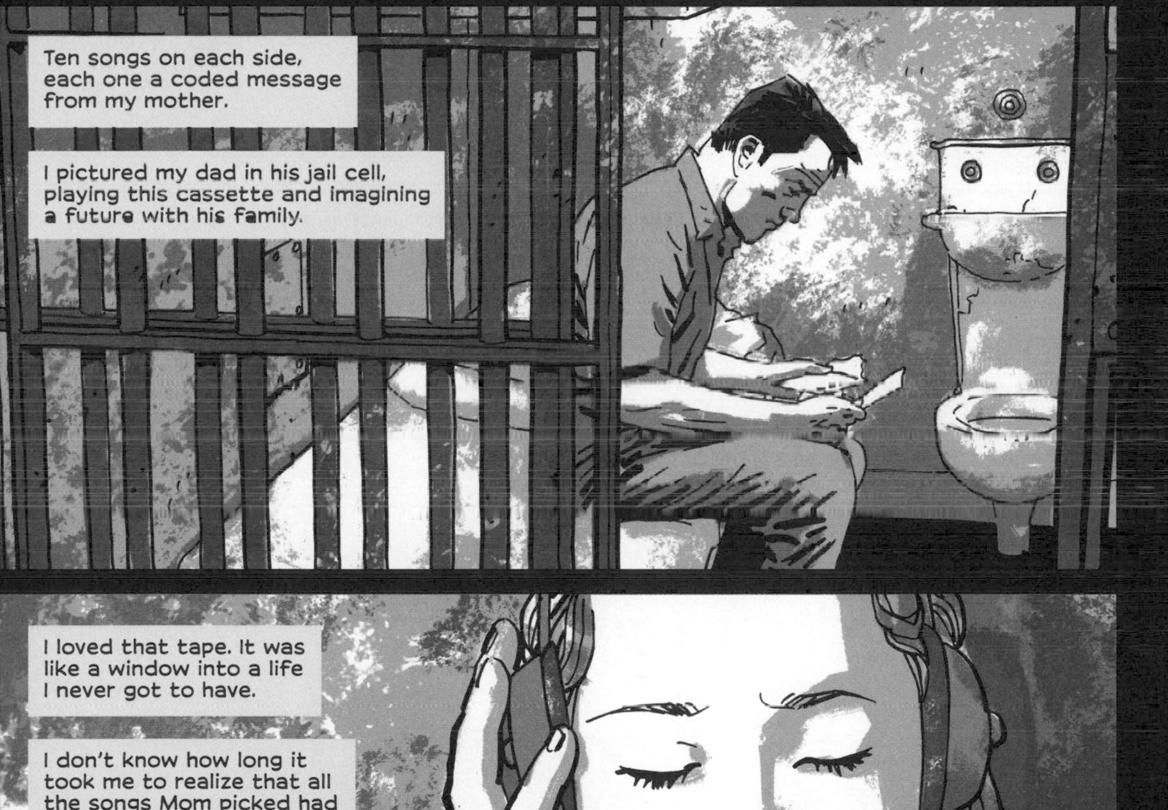
Ten songs on each side, each one a coded message from my mother.
I pictured my dad in his jail cell, playing this cassette and imagining a future with his family.

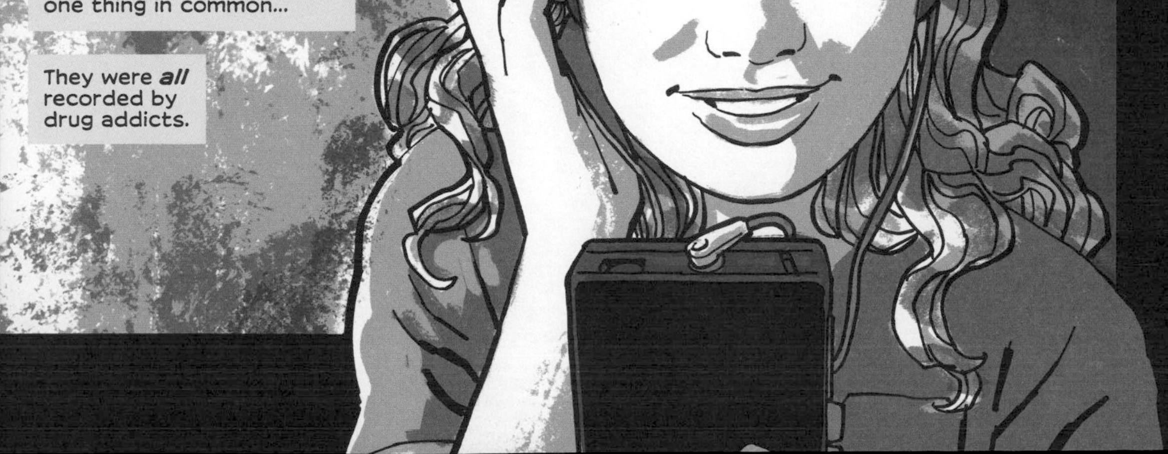
I loved that tape. It was like a window into a life I never got to have.
I don't know how long it took me to realize that all the songs Mom picked had one thing in common...
They were *all* recorded by drug addicts.

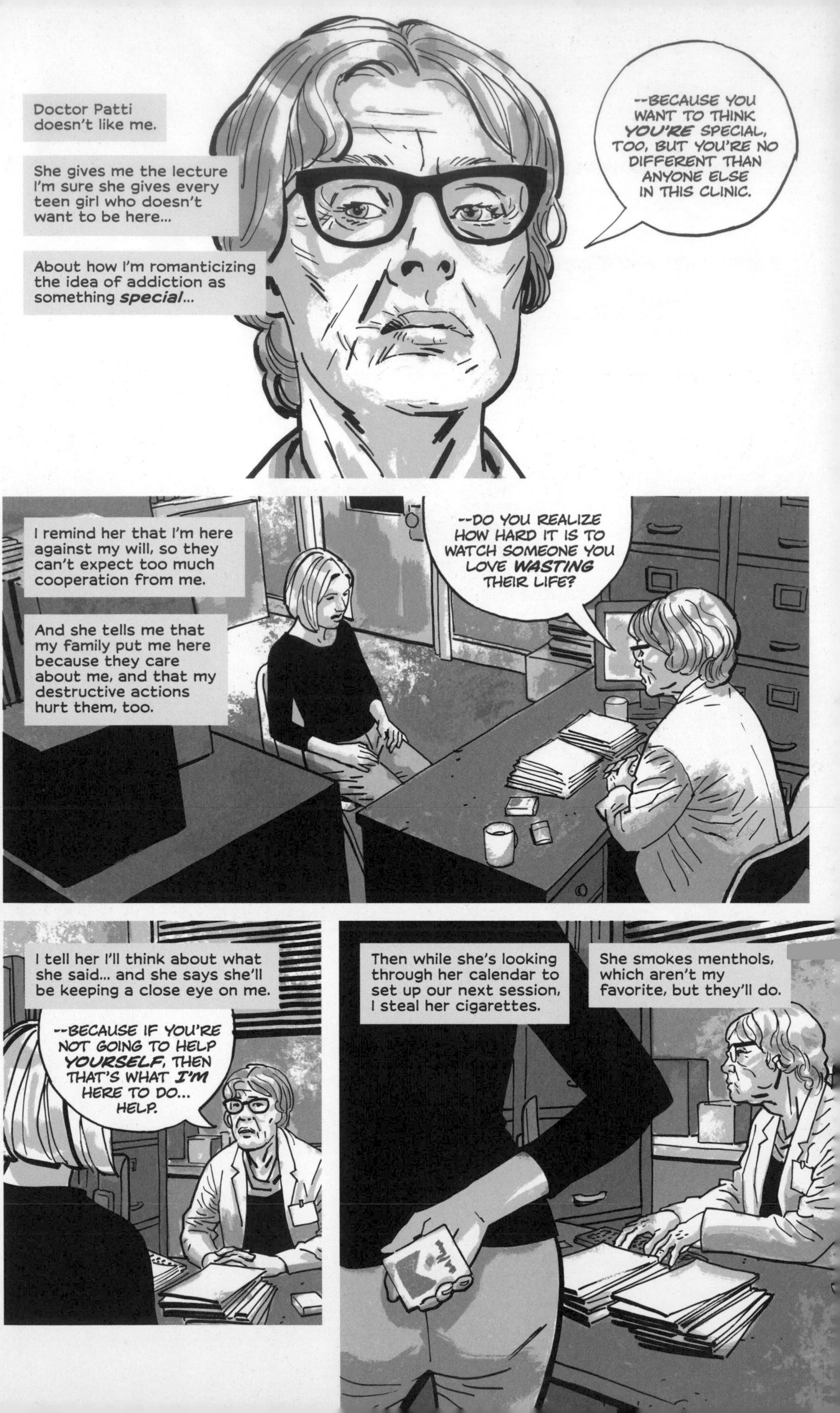
Doctor Patti doesn't like me.
She gives me the lecture I'm sure she gives every teen girl who doesn't want to be here...
About how I'm romanticizing the idea of addiction as something *special*...
--BECAUSE YOU WANT TO THINK ***YOU'RE*** SPECIAL, TOO, BUT YOU'RE NO DIFFERENT THAN ANYONE ELSE IN THIS CLINIC.
I remind her that I'm here against my will, so they can't expect too much cooperation from me.
And she tells me that my family put me here because they care about me, and that my destructive actions hurt them, too.
--DO YOU REALIZE HOW HARD IT IS TO WATCH SOMEONE YOU LOVE ***WASTING*** THEIR LIFE?
I tell her I'll think about what she said... and she says she'll be keeping a close eye on me.
--BECAUSE IF YOU'RE NOT GOING TO HELP ***YOURSELF***, THEN THAT'S WHAT ***I'M*** HERE TO DO... HELP.
Then while she's looking through her calendar to set up our next session, I steal her cigarettes.
She smokes menthols, which aren't my favorite, but they'll do.

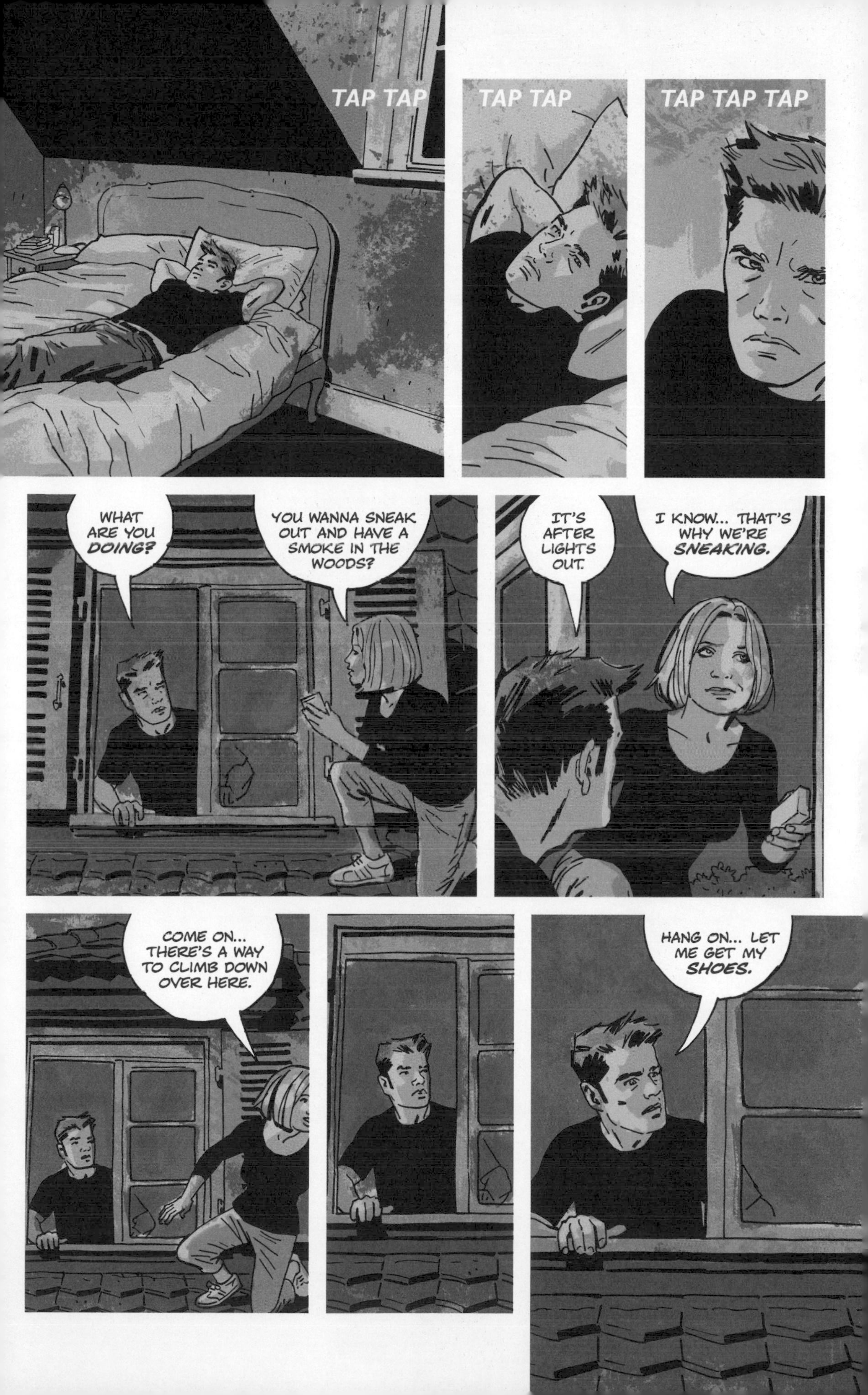
TAP TAP
TAP TAP
TAP TAP TAP
WHAT ARE YOU DOING?
YOU WANNA SNEAK OUT AND HAVE A SMOKE IN THE WOODS?
IT'S AFTER LIGHTS OUT.
I KNOW... THAT'S WHY WE'RE SNEAKING.
COME ON... THERE'S A WAY TO CLIMB DOWN OVER HERE.
HANG ON... LET ME GET MY SHOES.

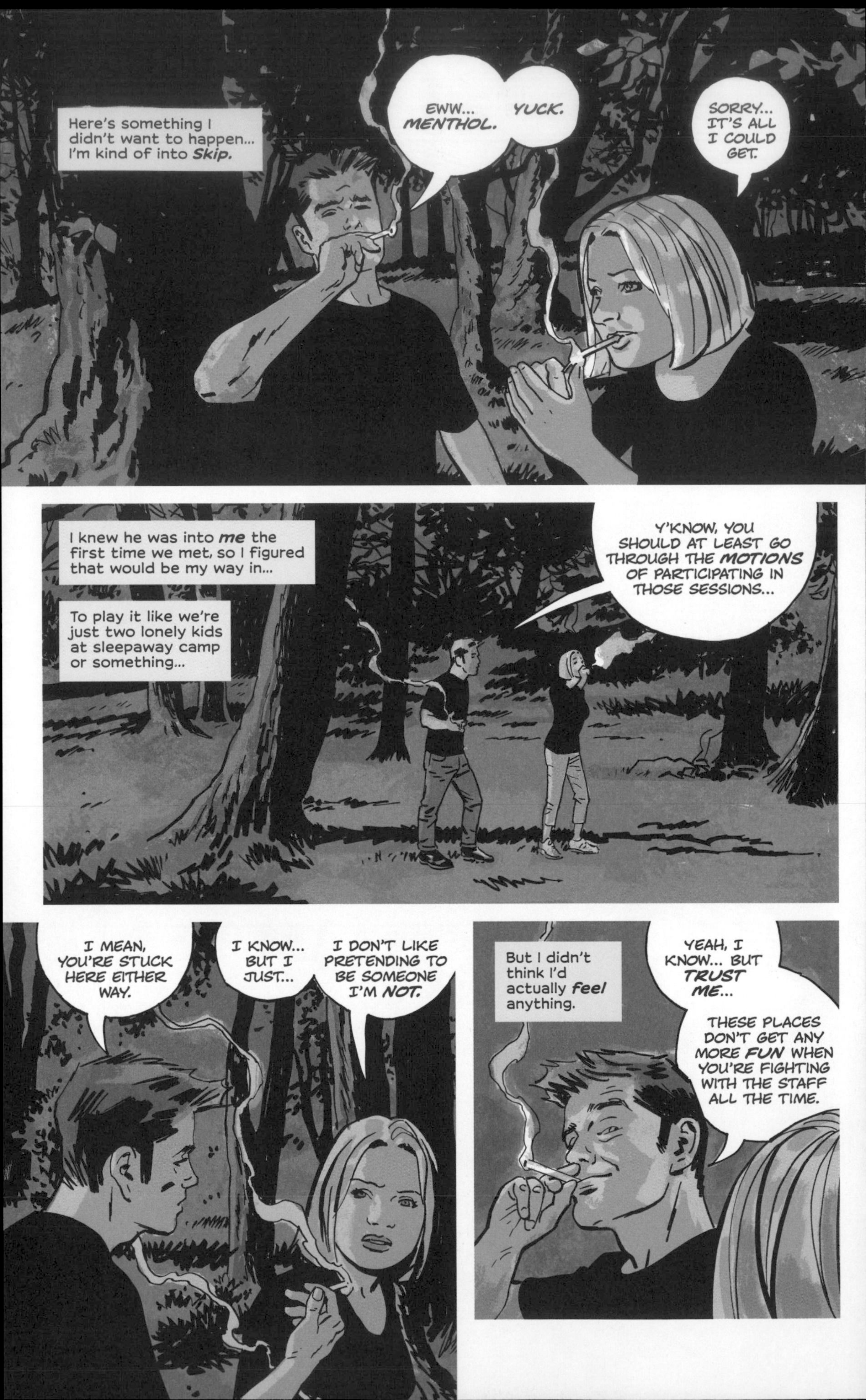

Here's something I didn't want to happen... I'm kind of into Skip.
EWW... MENTHOL.
YUCK.
SORRY... IT'S ALL I COULD GET.
I knew he was into me the first time we met, so I figured that would be my way in...
To play it like we're just two lonely kids at sleepaway camp or something...
Y'KNOW, YOU SHOULD AT LEAST GO THROUGH THE MOTIONS OF PARTICIPATING IN THOSE SESSIONS...
I MEAN, YOU'RE STUCK HERE EITHER WAY.
I KNOW... BUT I JUST...
I DON'T LIKE PRETENDING TO BE SOMEONE I'M NOT.
But I didn't think I'd actually feel anything.
YEAH, I KNOW... BUT TRUST ME...
THESE PLACES DON'T GET ANY MORE FUN WHEN YOU'RE FIGHTING WITH THE STAFF ALL THE TIME.

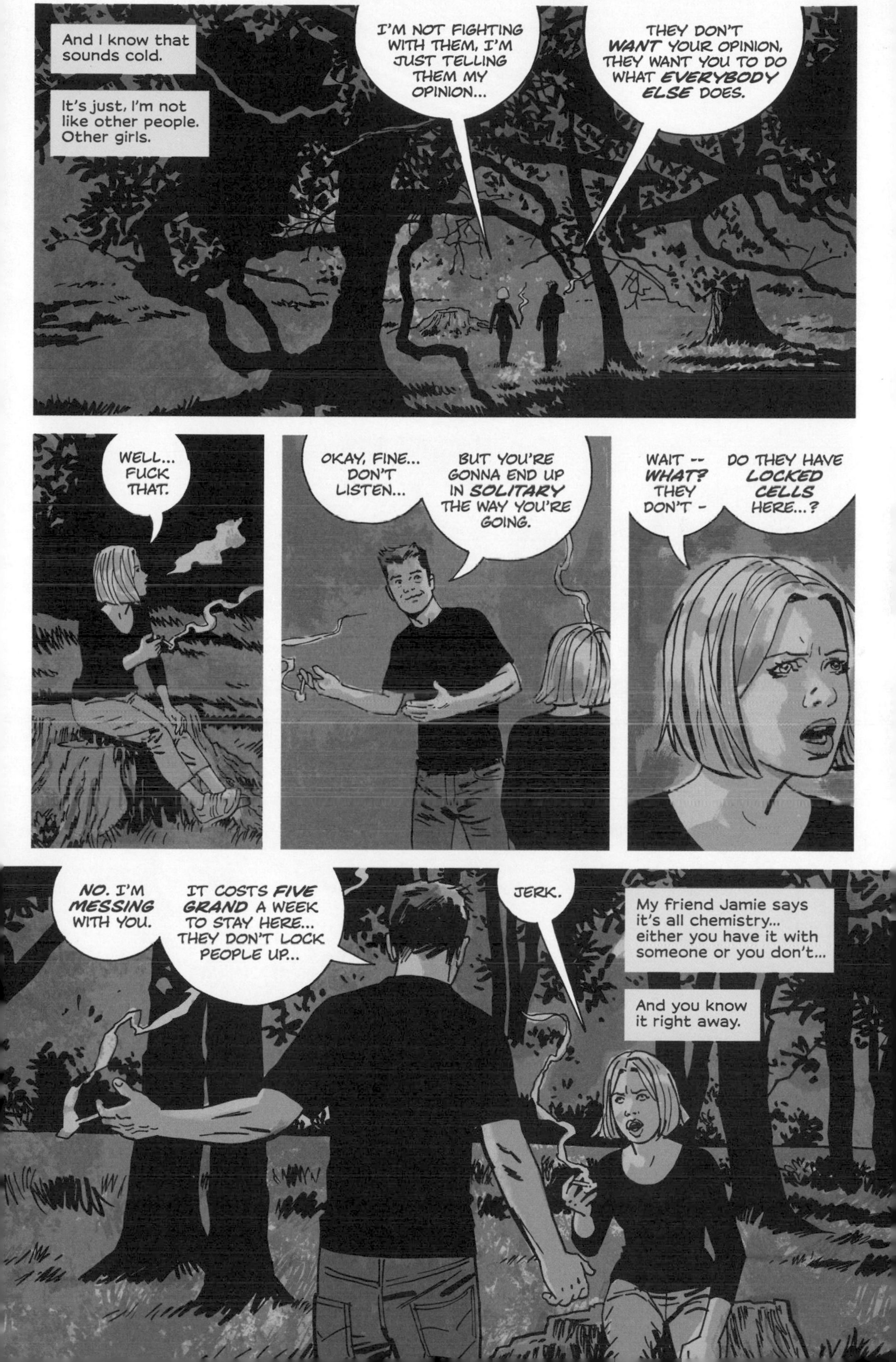
And I know that sounds cold.
It's just, I'm not like other people. Other girls.
I'M NOT FIGHTING WITH THEM, I'M JUST TELLING THEM MY OPINION...
THEY DON'T WANT YOUR OPINION, THEY WANT YOU TO DO WHAT EVERYBODY ELSE DOES.
WELL... FUCK THAT.
OKAY, FINE... DON'T LISTEN...
BUT YOU'RE GONNA END UP IN SOLITARY THE WAY YOU'RE GOING.
WAIT -- WHAT? THEY DON'T -
DO THEY HAVE LOCKED CELLS HERE...?
NO. I'M MESSING WITH YOU.
IT COSTS FIVE GRAND A WEEK TO STAY HERE... THEY DON'T LOCK PEOPLE UP...
JERK.
My friend Jamie says it's all chemistry... either you have it with someone or you don't...
And you know it right away.

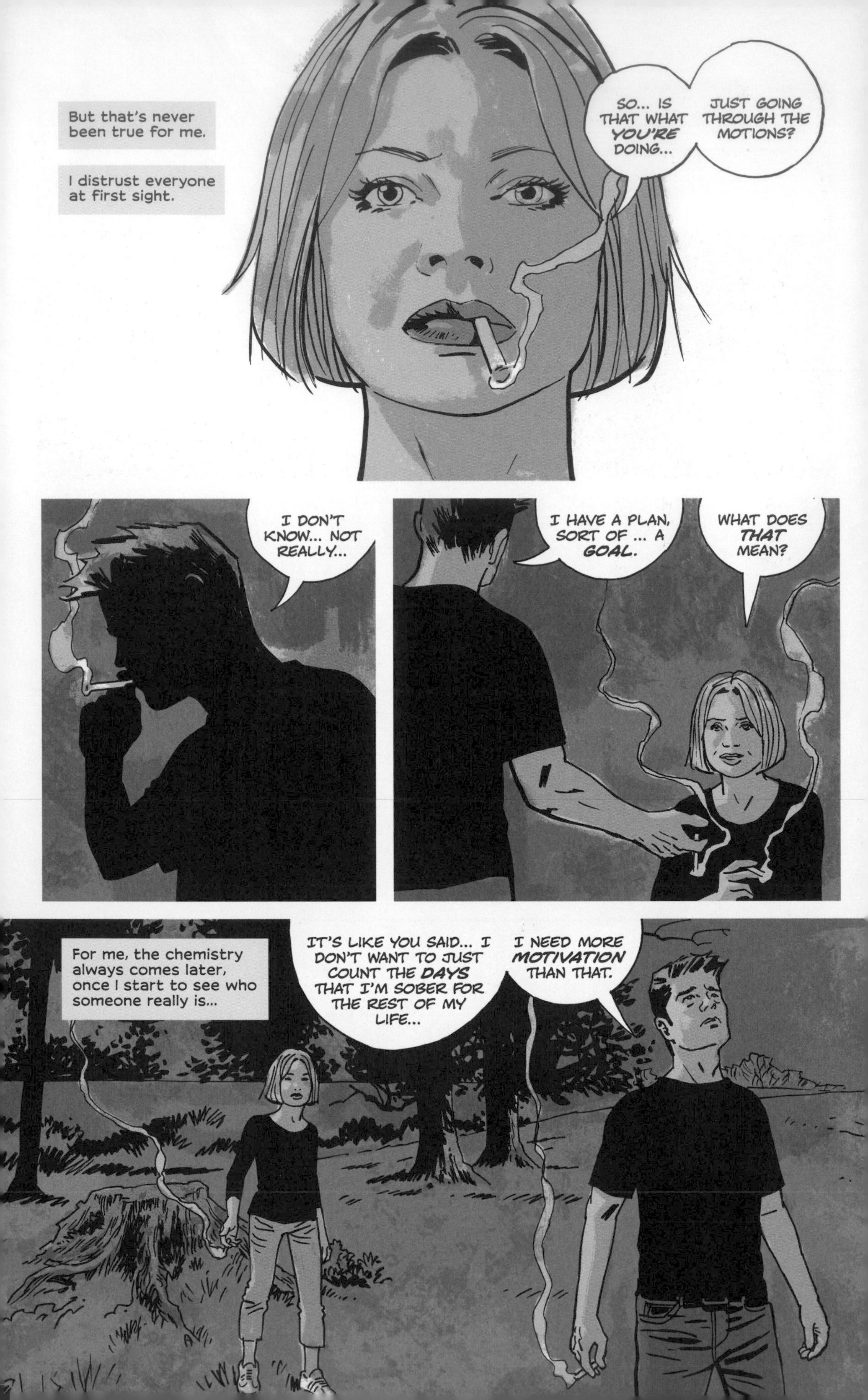
But that's never been true for me.
I distrust everyone at first sight.
SO... IS THAT WHAT YOU'RE DOING...
JUST GOING THROUGH THE MOTIONS?
I DON'T KNOW... NOT REALLY...
I HAVE A PLAN, SORT OF ... A GOAL.
WHAT DOES THAT MEAN?
For me, the chemistry always comes later, once I start to see who someone really is...
IT'S LIKE YOU SAID... I DON'T WANT TO JUST COUNT THE DAYS THAT I'M SOBER FOR THE REST OF MY LIFE...
I NEED MORE MOTIVATION THAN THAT.

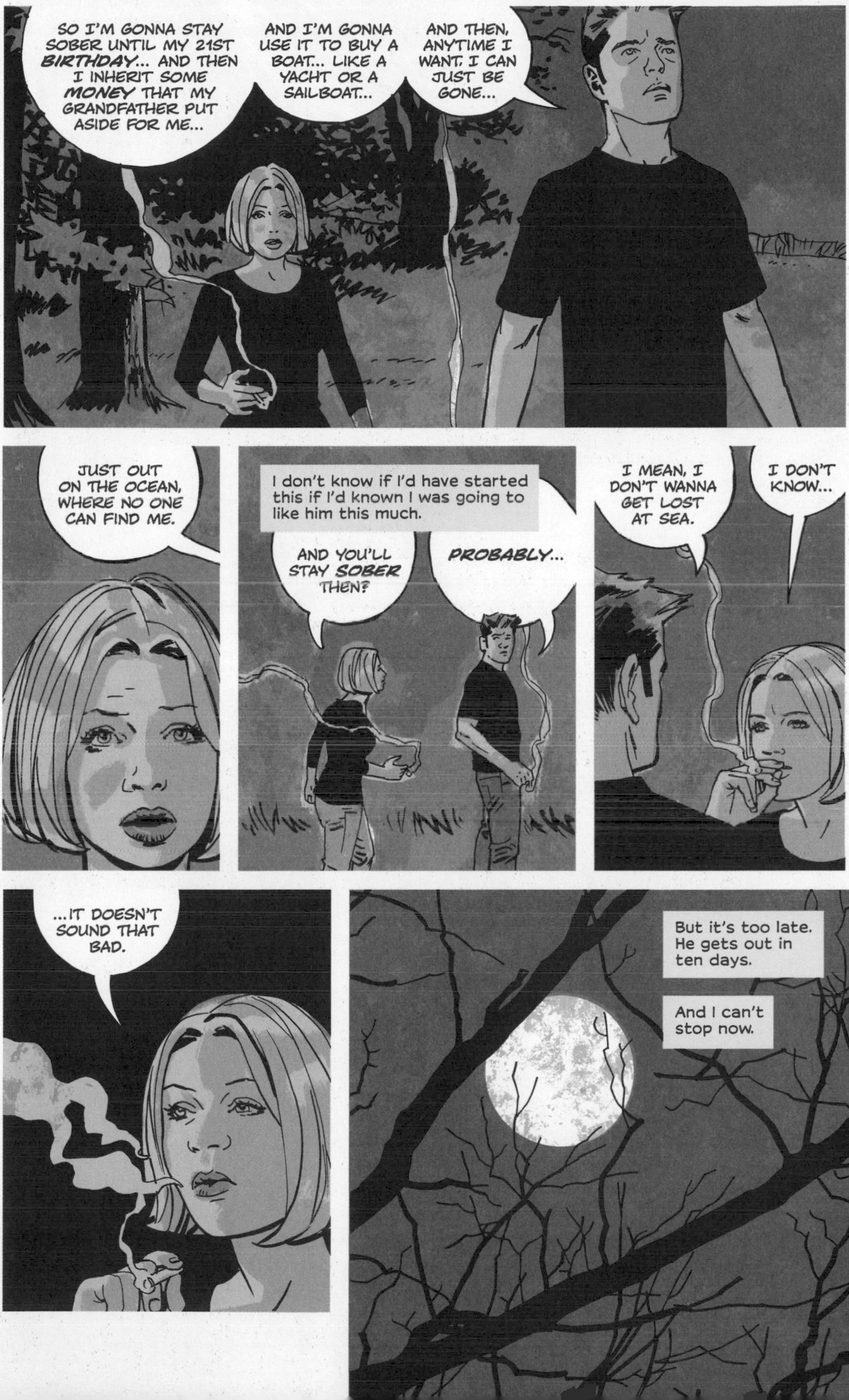
SO I'M GONNA STAY SOBER UNTIL MY 21ST *BIRTHDAY*... AND THEN I INHERIT SOME *MONEY* THAT MY GRANDFATHER PUT ASIDE FOR ME...
AND I'M GONNA USE IT TO BUY A BOAT... LIKE A YACHT OR A SAILBOAT...
AND THEN, ANYTIME I WANT, I CAN JUST BE GONE...
JUST OUT ON THE OCEAN, WHERE NO ONE CAN FIND ME.
I don't know if I'd have started this if I'd known I was going to like him this much.
AND YOU'LL STAY *SOBER* THEN?
PROBABLY...
I MEAN, I DON'T WANNA GET LOST AT SEA.
I DON'T KNOW...
...IT DOESN'T SOUND THAT BAD.
But it's too late. He gets out in ten days.
And I can't stop now.

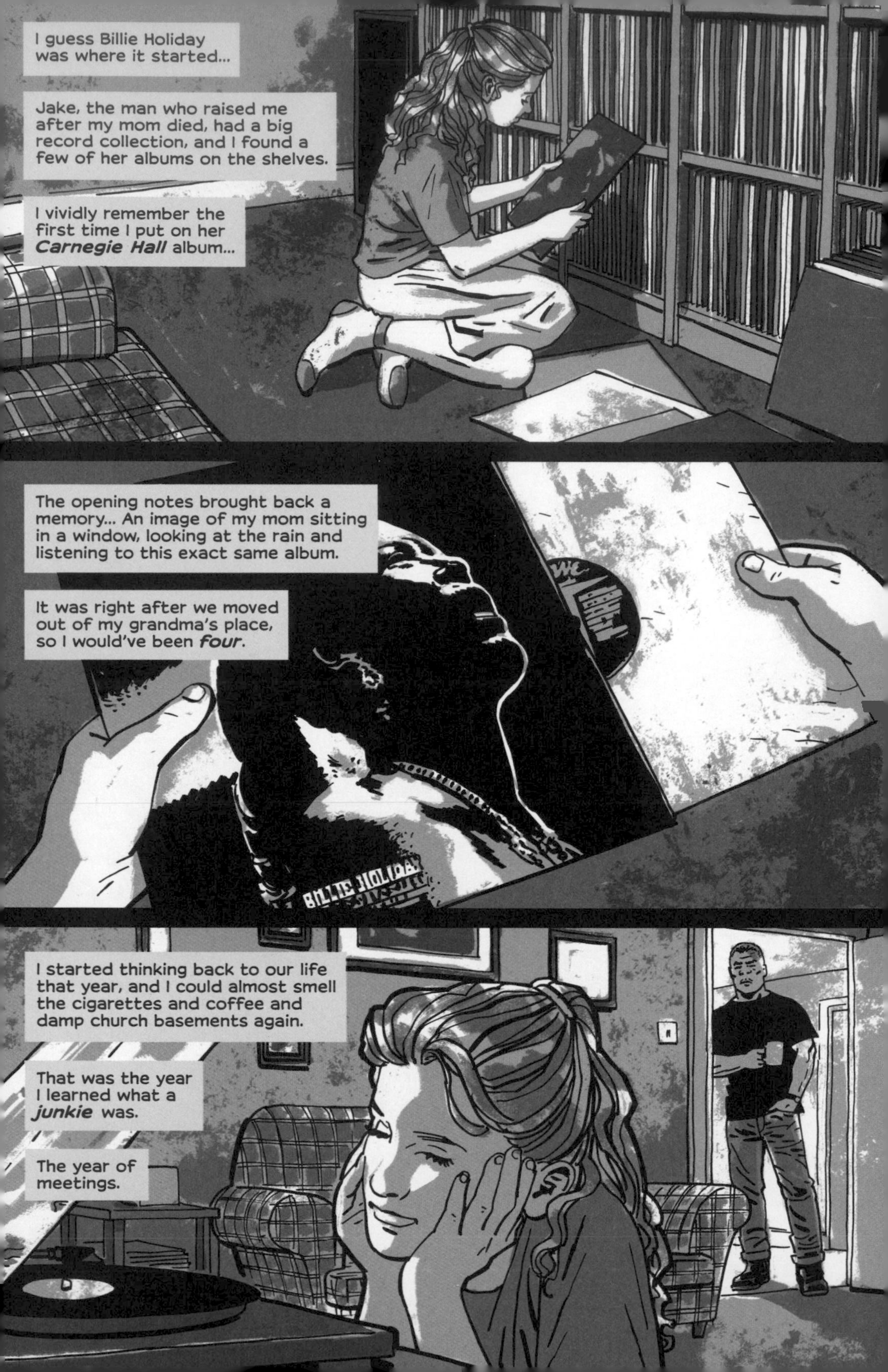
I guess Billie Holiday was where it started...
Jake, the man who raised me after my mom died, had a big record collection, and I found a few of her albums on the shelves.
I vividly remember the first time I put on her *Carnegie Hall* album...
The opening notes brought back a memory... An image of my mom sitting in a window, looking at the rain and listening to this exact same album.
It was right after we moved out of my grandma's place, so I would've been *four*.
I started thinking back to our life that year, and I could almost smell the cigarettes and coffee and damp church basements again.
That was the year I learned what a *junkie* was.
The year of meetings.

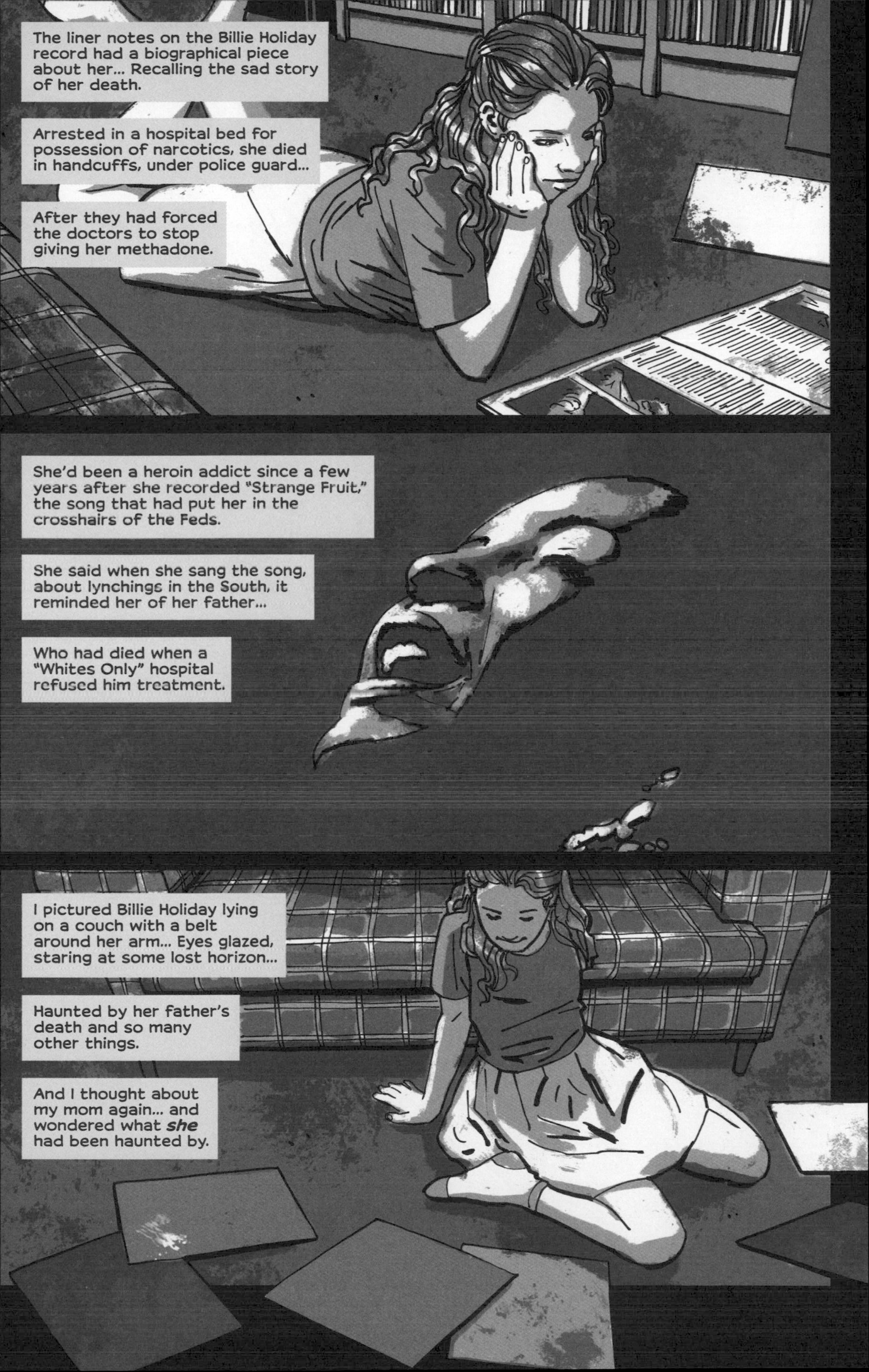

The liner notes on the Billie Holiday record had a biographical piece about her... Recalling the sad story of her death.
Arrested in a hospital bed for possession of narcotics, she died in handcuffs, under police guard...
After they had forced the doctors to stop giving her methadone.
She'd been a heroin addict since a few years after she recorded "Strange Fruit," the song that had put her in the crosshairs of the Feds.
She said when she sang the song, about lynchings in the South, it reminded her of her father...
Who had died when a "Whites Only" hospital refused him treatment.
I pictured Billie Holiday lying on a couch with a belt around her arm... Eyes glazed, staring at some lost horizon...
Haunted by her father's death and so many other things.
And I thought about my mom again... and wondered what *she* had been haunted by.

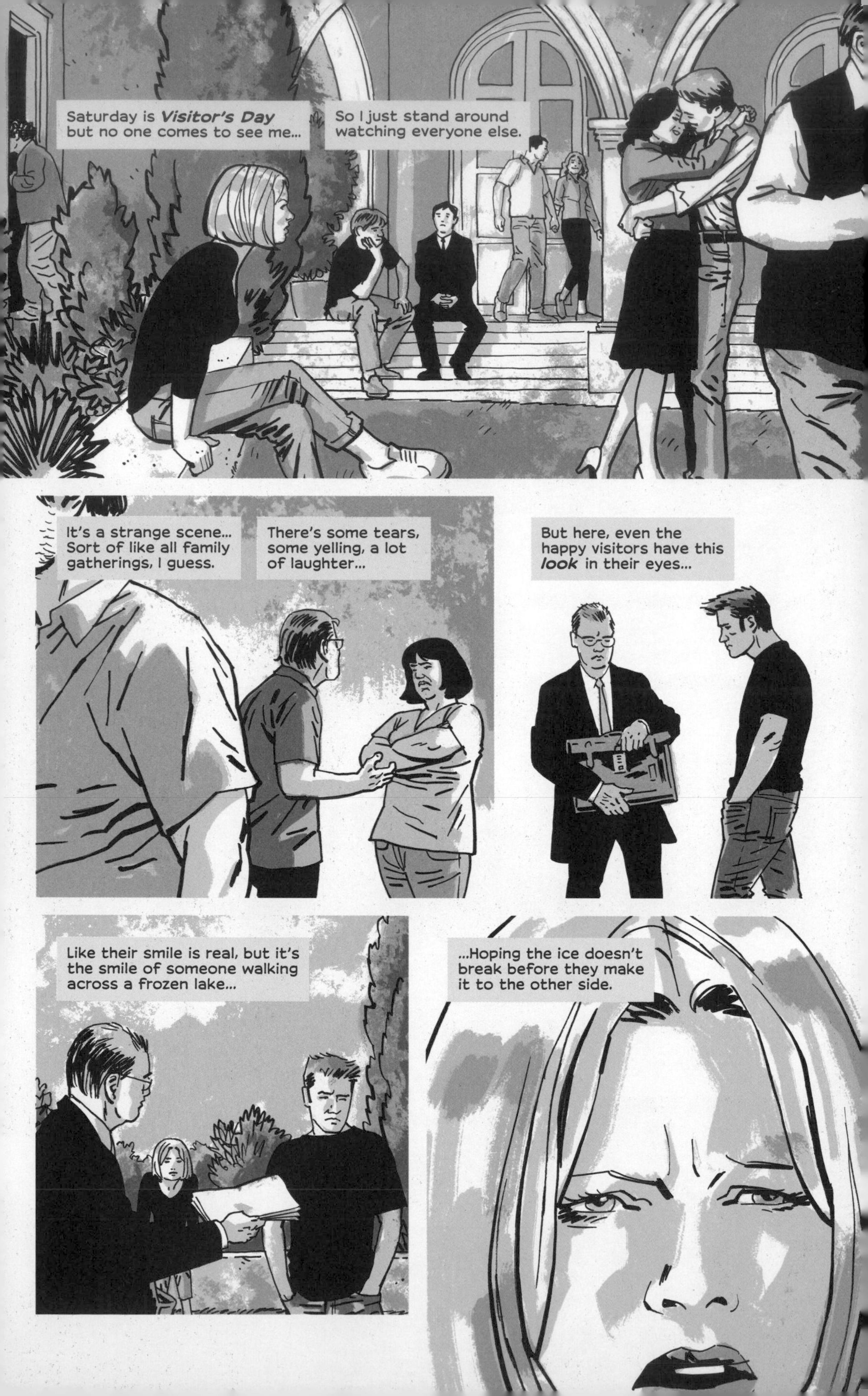
Saturday is *Visitor's Day* but no one comes to see me...
So I just stand around watching everyone else.
It's a strange scene... Sort of like all family gatherings, I guess.
There's some tears, some yelling, a lot of laughter...
But here, even the happy visitors have this *look* in their eyes...
Like their smile is real, but it's the smile of someone walking across a frozen lake...
...Hoping the ice doesn't break before they make it to the other side.

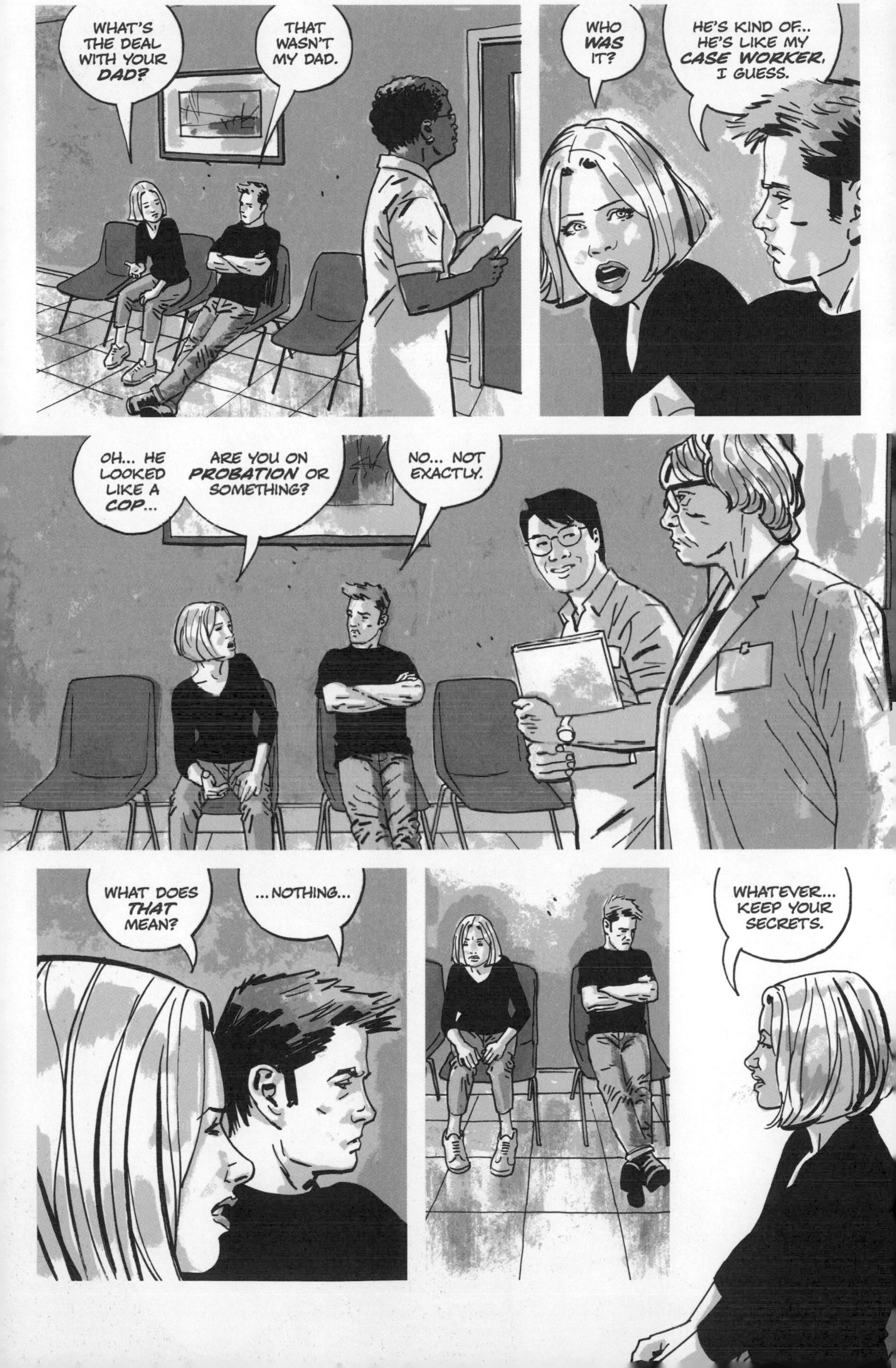
WHAT'S THE DEAL WITH YOUR DAD?
THAT WASN'T MY DAD.
WHO WAS IT?
HE'S KIND OF... HE'S LIKE MY CASE WORKER, I GUESS.
OH... HE LOOKED LIKE A COP...
ARE YOU ON PROBATION OR SOMETHING?
NO... NOT EXACTLY.
WHAT DOES THAT MEAN?
...NOTHING...
WHATEVER... KEEP YOUR SECRETS.

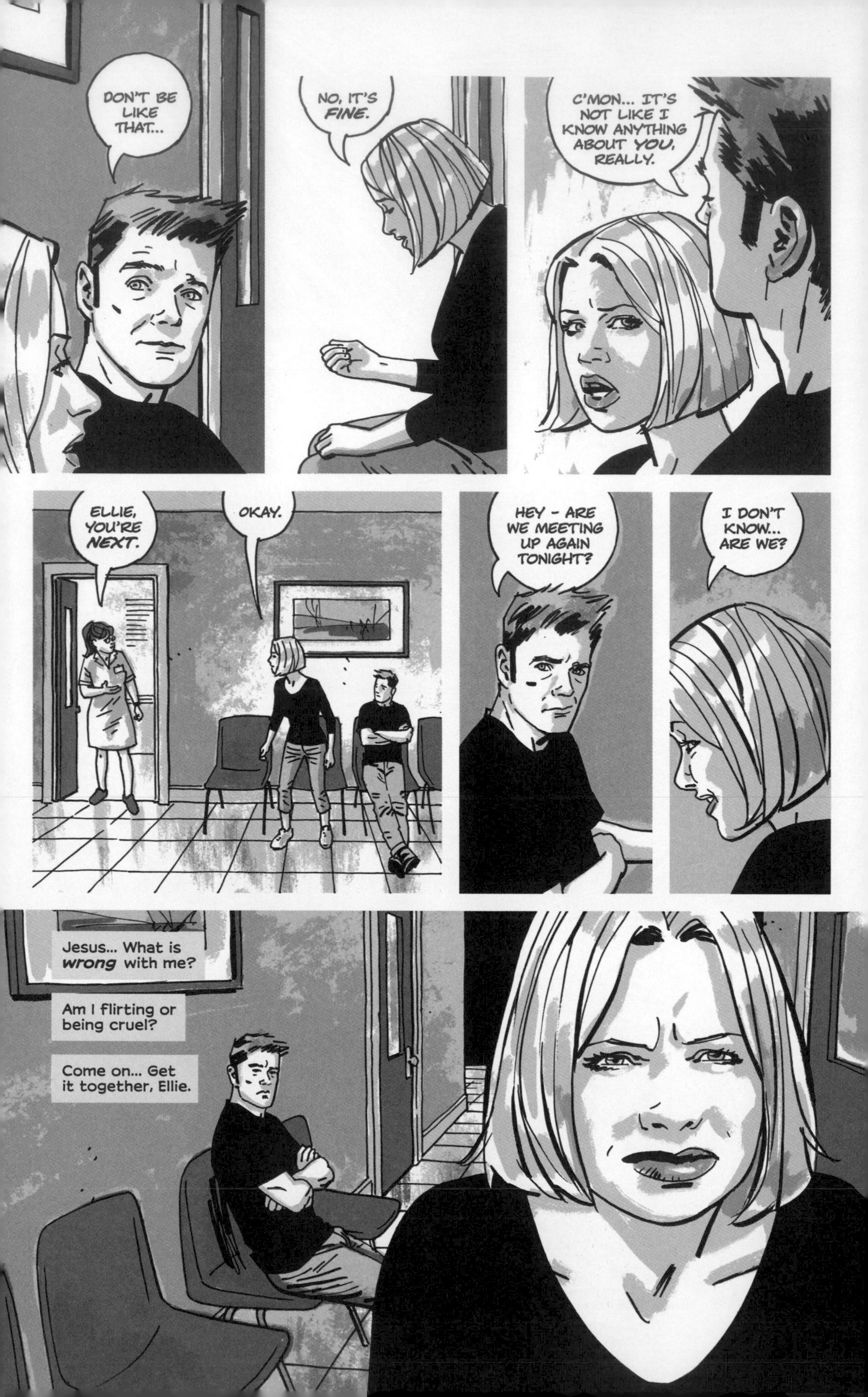
DON'T BE LIKE THAT...
NO, IT'S FINE.
C'MON... IT'S NOT LIKE I KNOW ANYTHING ABOUT YOU, REALLY.
ELLIE, YOU'RE NEXT.
OKAY.
HEY - ARE WE MEETING UP AGAIN TONIGHT?
I DON'T KNOW... ARE WE?
Jesus... What is wrong with me?
Am I flirting or being cruel?
Come on... Get it together, Ellie.

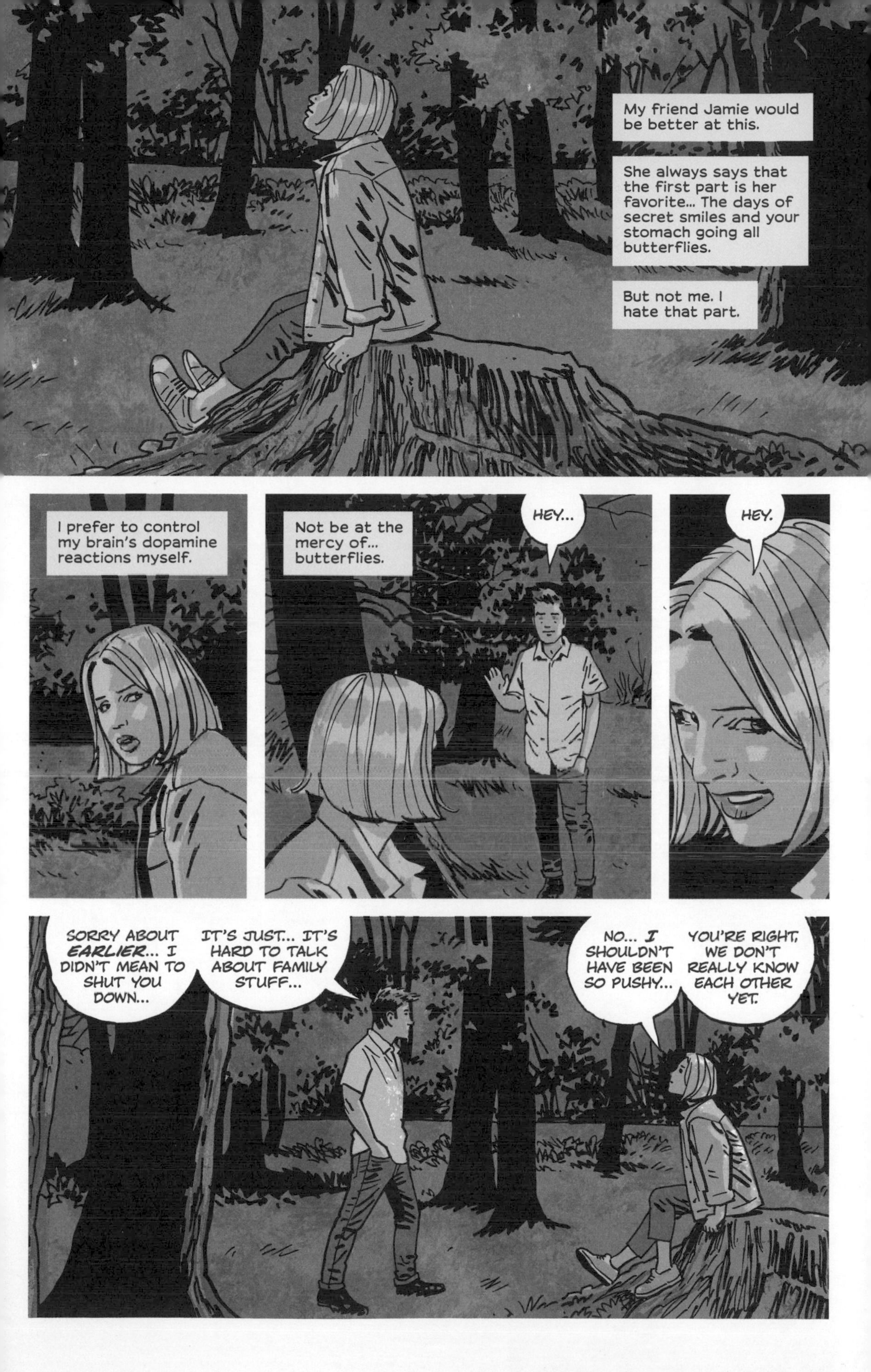

My friend Jamie would be better at this.
She always says that the first part is her favorite... The days of secret smiles and your stomach going all butterflies.
But not me. I hate that part.
I prefer to control my brain's dopamine reactions myself.
Not be at the mercy of... butterflies.
HEY...
HEY.
SORRY ABOUT *EARLIER*... I DIDN'T MEAN TO SHUT YOU DOWN...
IT'S JUST... IT'S HARD TO TALK ABOUT FAMILY STUFF...
NO... *I* SHOULDN'T HAVE BEEN SO PUSHY...
YOU'RE RIGHT, WE DON'T REALLY KNOW EACH OTHER YET.

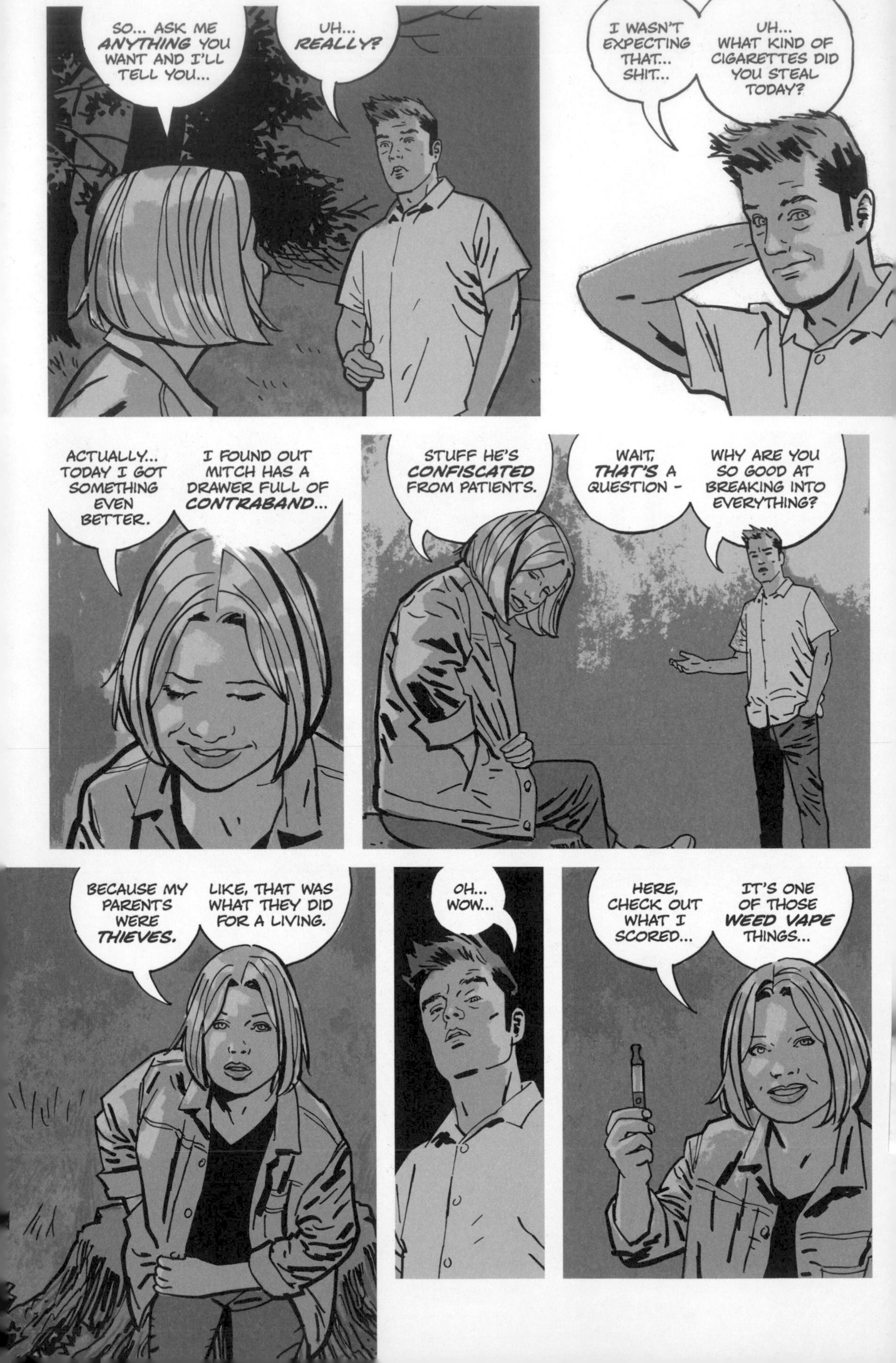
SO... ASK ME ANYTHING YOU WANT AND I'LL TELL YOU...
UH... REALLY?
I WASN'T EXPECTING THAT... SHIT...
UH... WHAT KIND OF CIGARETTES DID YOU STEAL TODAY?
ACTUALLY... TODAY I GOT SOMETHING EVEN BETTER.
I FOUND OUT MITCH HAS A DRAWER FULL OF CONTRABAND...
STUFF HE'S CONFISCATED FROM PATIENTS.
WAIT, THAT'S A QUESTION -
WHY ARE YOU SO GOOD AT BREAKING INTO EVERYTHING?
BECAUSE MY PARENTS WERE THIEVES.
LIKE, THAT WAS WHAT THEY DID FOR A LIVING.
OH... WOW...
HERE, CHECK OUT WHAT I SCORED...
IT'S ONE OF THOSE WEED VAPE THINGS...

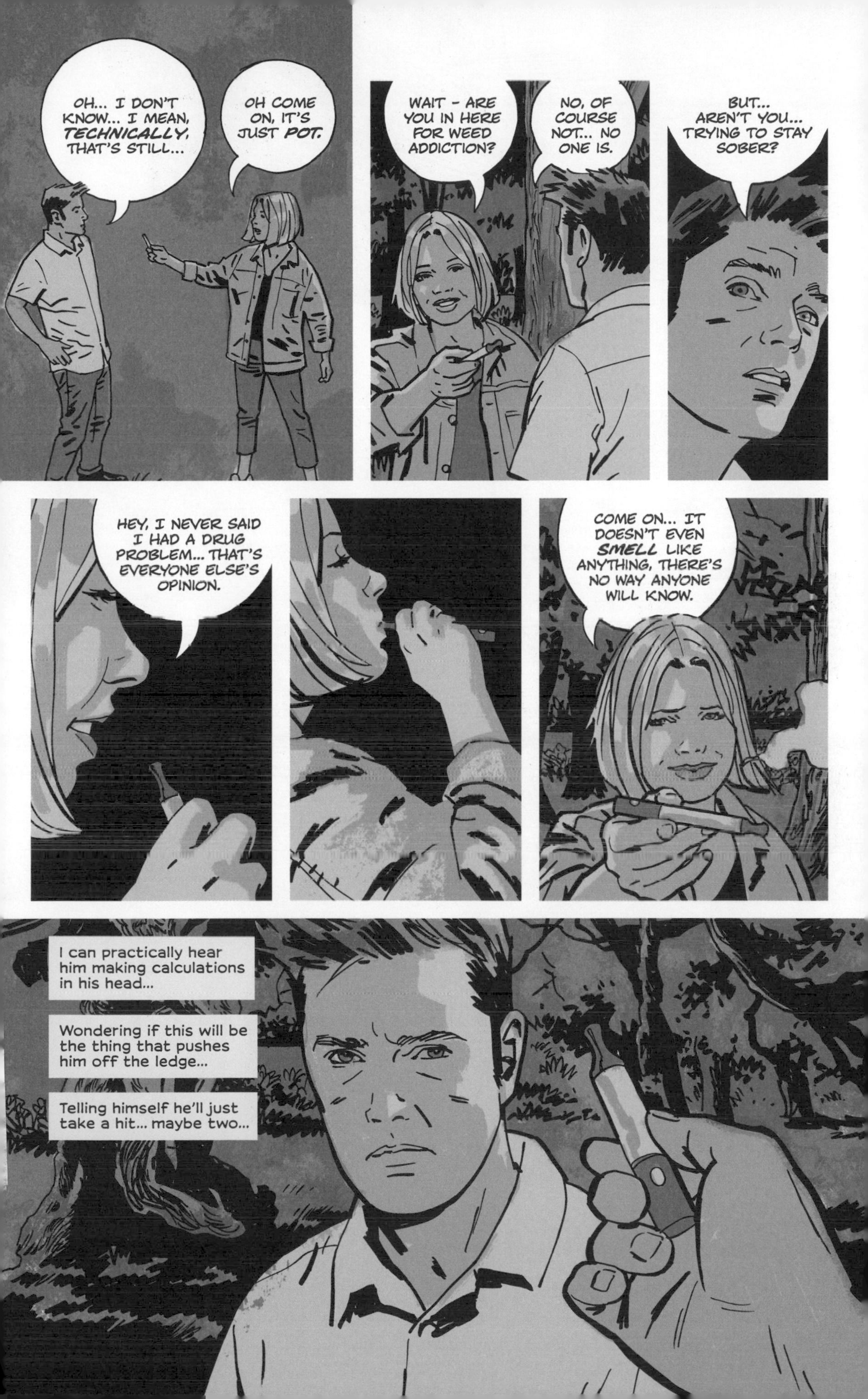
OH... I DON'T KNOW... I MEAN, TECHNICALLY, THAT'S STILL...
OH COME ON, IT'S JUST POT.
WAIT - ARE YOU IN HERE FOR WEED ADDICTION?
NO, OF COURSE NOT... NO ONE IS.
BUT... AREN'T YOU... TRYING TO STAY SOBER?
HEY, I NEVER SAID I HAD A DRUG PROBLEM... THAT'S EVERYONE ELSE'S OPINION.
COME ON... IT DOESN'T EVEN SMELL LIKE ANYTHING, THERE'S NO WAY ANYONE WILL KNOW.
I can practically hear him making calculations in his head...
Wondering if this will be the thing that pushes him off the ledge...
Telling himself he'll just take a hit... maybe two...

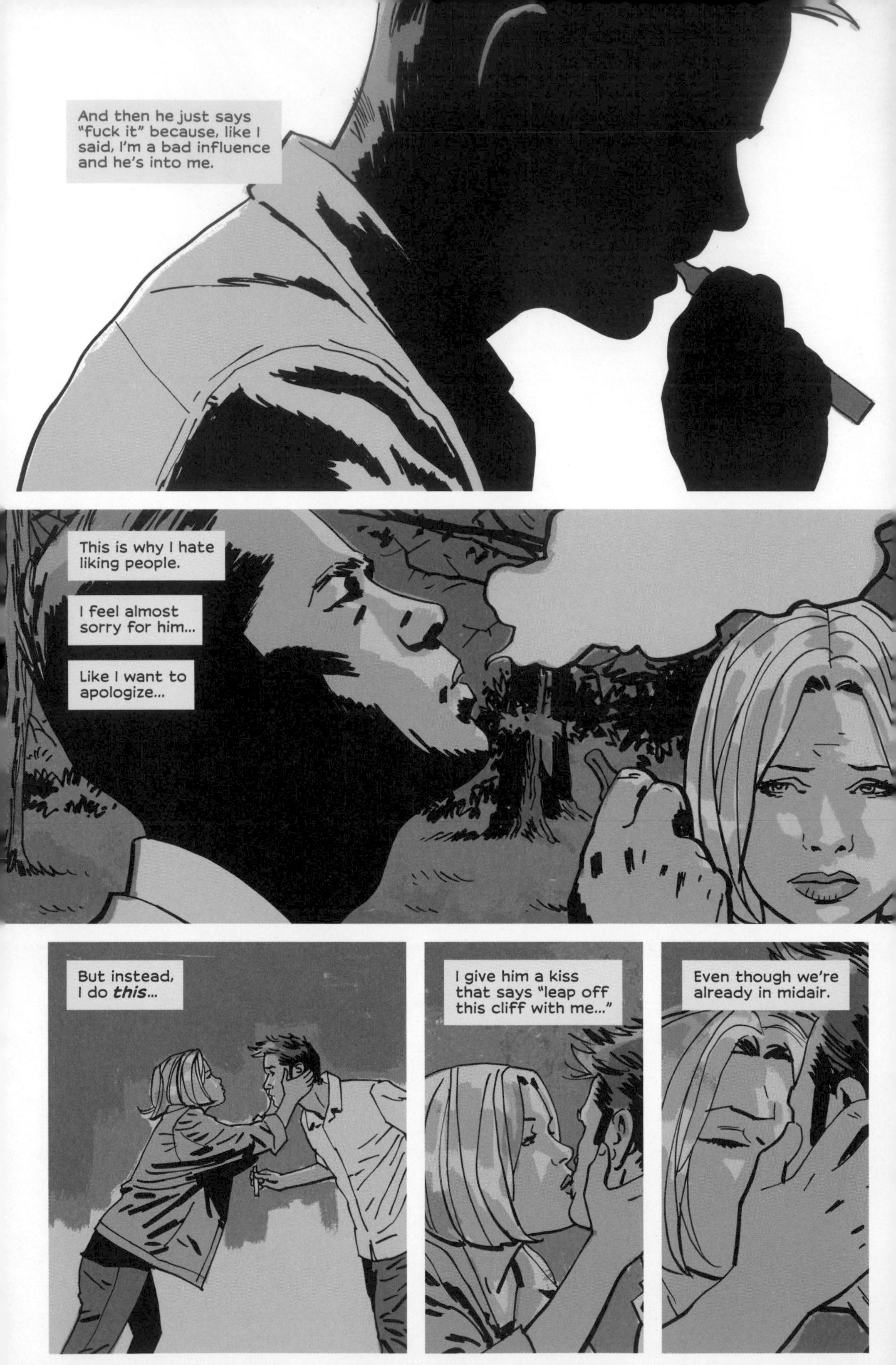
And then he just says "fuck it" because, like I said, I'm a bad influence and he's into me.
This is why I hate liking people.
I feel almost sorry for him...
Like I want to apologize...
But instead, I do *this*...
I give him a kiss that says "leap off this cliff with me..."
Even though we're already in midair.

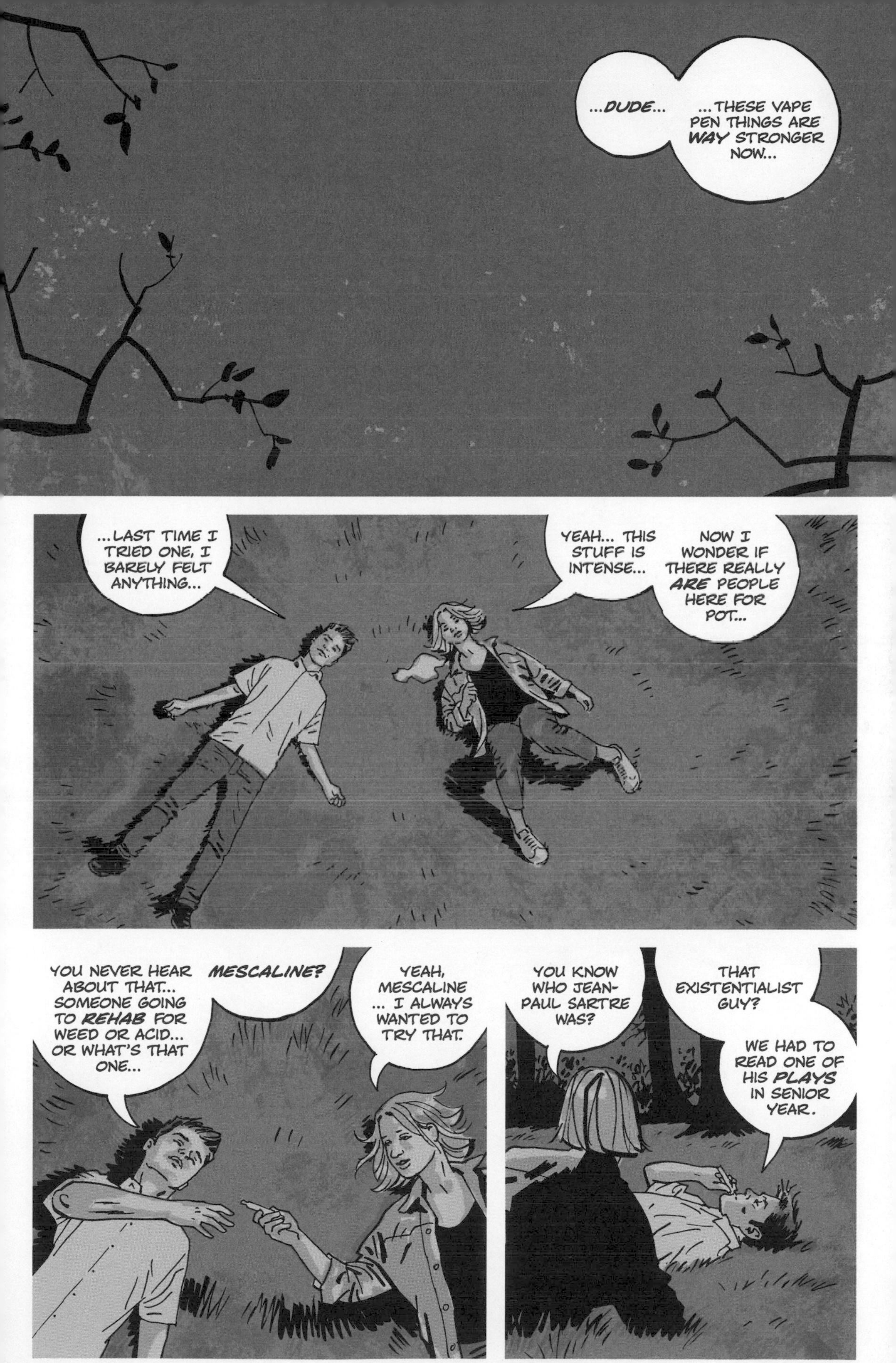
...DUDE...
...THESE VAPE PEN THINGS ARE WAY STRONGER NOW...
...LAST TIME I TRIED ONE, I BARELY FELT ANYTHING...
YEAH... THIS STUFF IS INTENSE...
NOW I WONDER IF THERE REALLY ARE PEOPLE HERE FOR POT...
YOU NEVER HEAR ABOUT THAT... SOMEONE GOING TO REHAB FOR WEED OR ACID... OR WHAT'S THAT ONE...
MESCALINE?
YEAH, MESCALINE ... I ALWAYS WANTED TO TRY THAT.
YOU KNOW WHO JEAN-PAUL SARTRE WAS?
THAT EXISTENTIALIST GUY?
WE HAD TO READ ONE OF HIS PLAYS IN SENIOR YEAR.

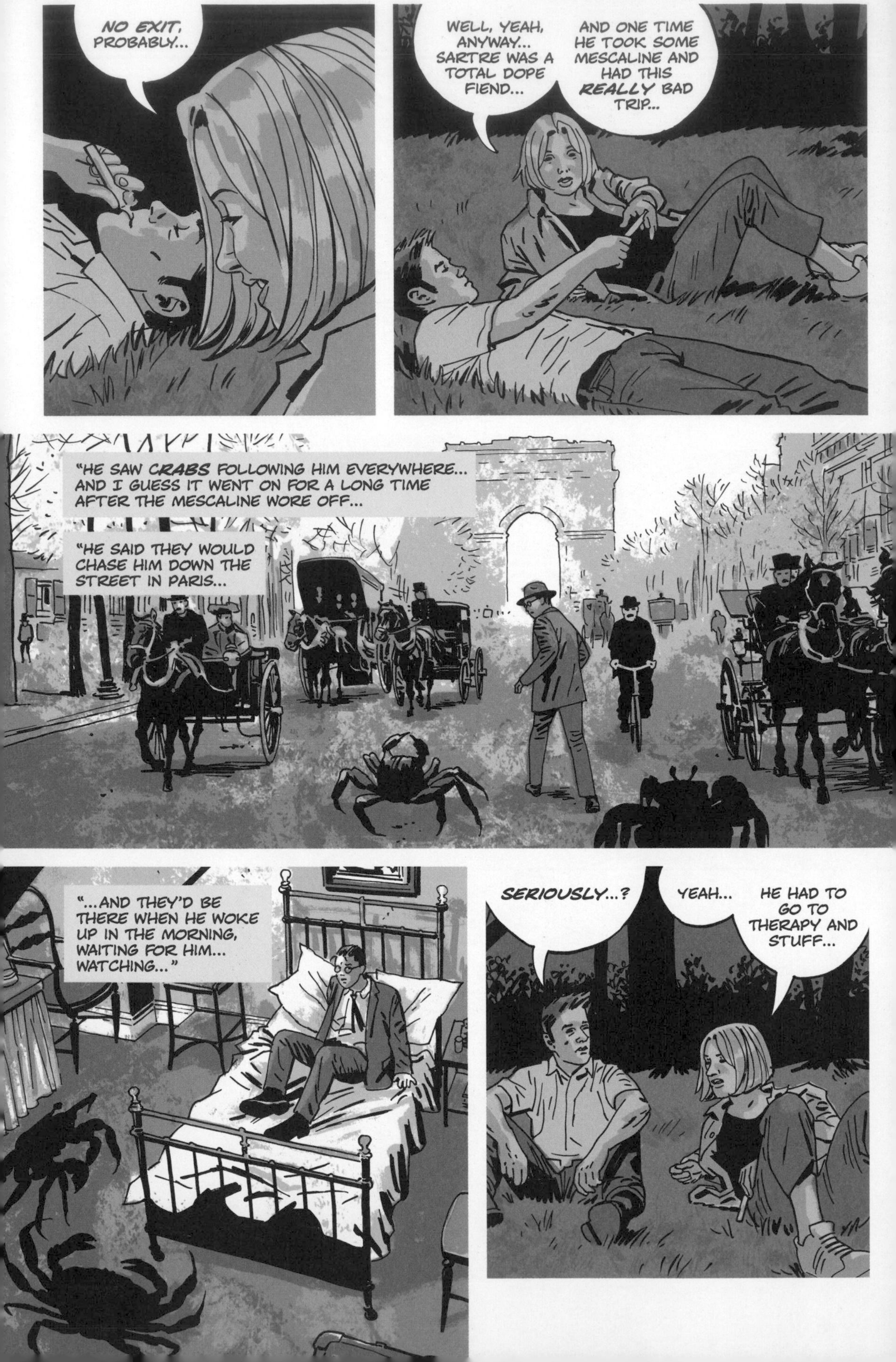
NO EXIT, PROBABLY...
WELL, YEAH, ANYWAY... SARTRE WAS A TOTAL DOPE FIEND...
AND ONE TIME HE TOOK SOME MESCALINE AND HAD THIS REALLY BAD TRIP...
"HE SAW CRABS FOLLOWING HIM EVERYWHERE... AND I GUESS IT WENT ON FOR A LONG TIME AFTER THE MESCALINE WORE OFF...
"HE SAID THEY WOULD CHASE HIM DOWN THE STREET IN PARIS...
"...AND THEY'D BE THERE WHEN HE WOKE UP IN THE MORNING, WAITING FOR HIM... WATCHING..."
SERIOUSLY...?
YEAH...
HE HAD TO GO TO THERAPY AND STUFF...

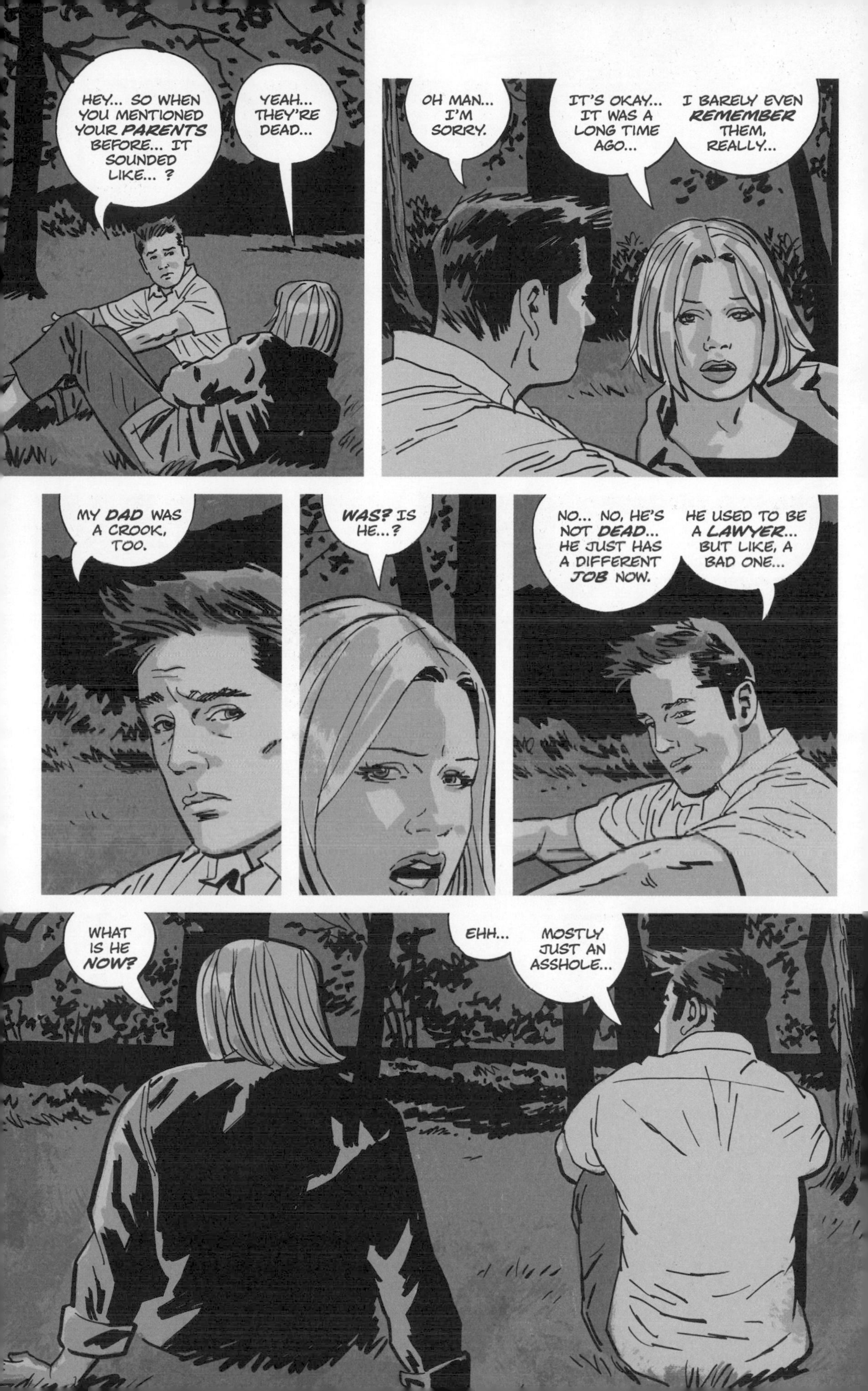
HEY... SO WHEN YOU MENTIONED YOUR PARENTS BEFORE... IT SOUNDED LIKE... ?
YEAH... THEY'RE DEAD...
OH MAN... I'M SORRY.
IT'S OKAY... IT WAS A LONG TIME AGO...
I BARELY EVEN REMEMBER THEM, REALLY...
MY DAD WAS A CROOK, TOO.
WAS? IS HE...?
NO... NO, HE'S NOT DEAD... HE JUST HAS A DIFFERENT JOB NOW.
HE USED TO BE A LAWYER... BUT LIKE, A BAD ONE...
WHAT IS HE NOW?
EHH...
MOSTLY JUST AN ASSHOLE...

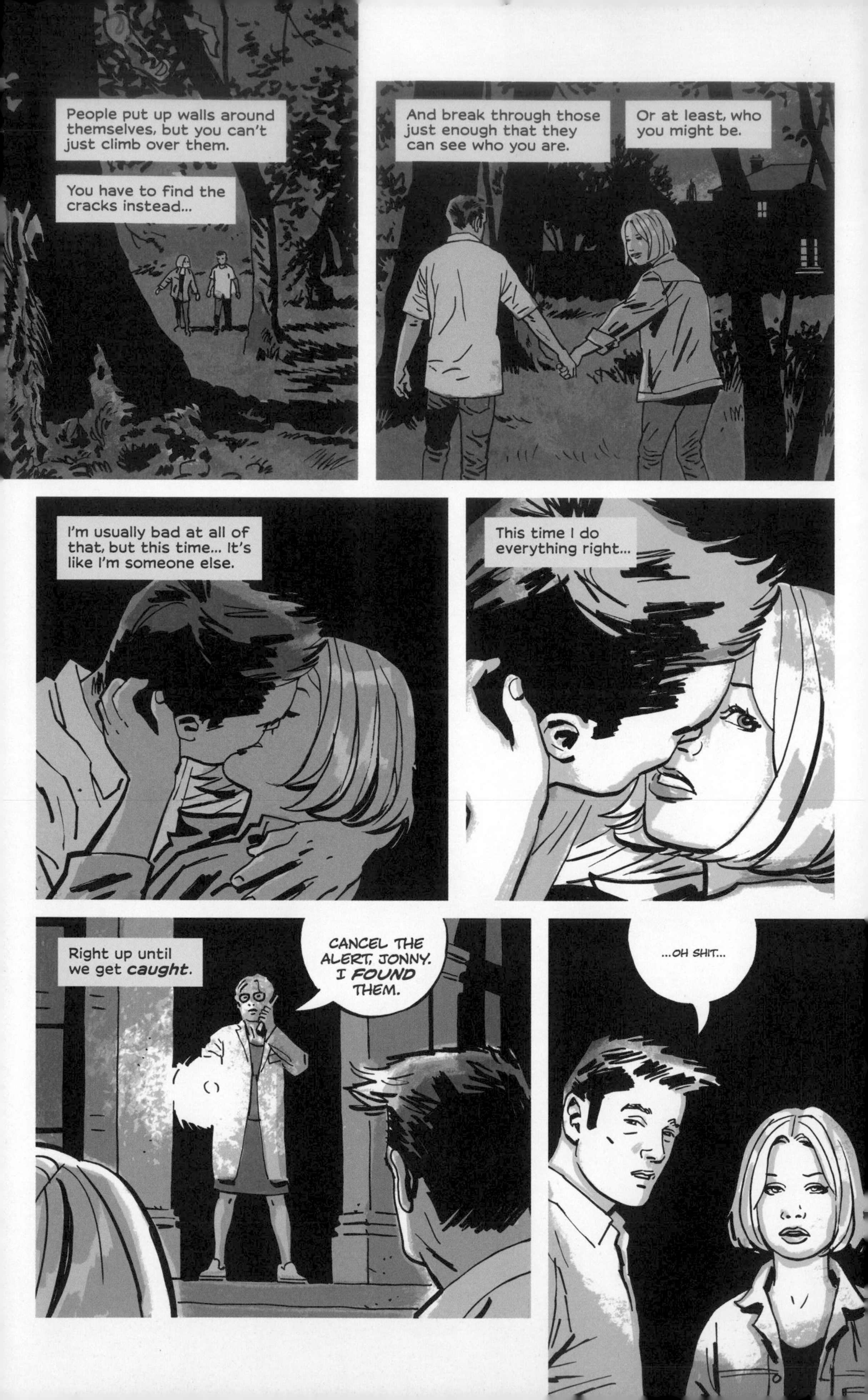
People put up walls around themselves, but you can't just climb over them.
You have to find the cracks instead...
And break through those just enough that they can see who you are.
Or at least, who you might be.
I'm usually bad at all of that, but this time... It's like I'm someone else.
This time I do everything right...
Right up until we get *caught*.
CANCEL THE ALERT, JONNY. I *FOUND* THEM.
...OH SHIT...

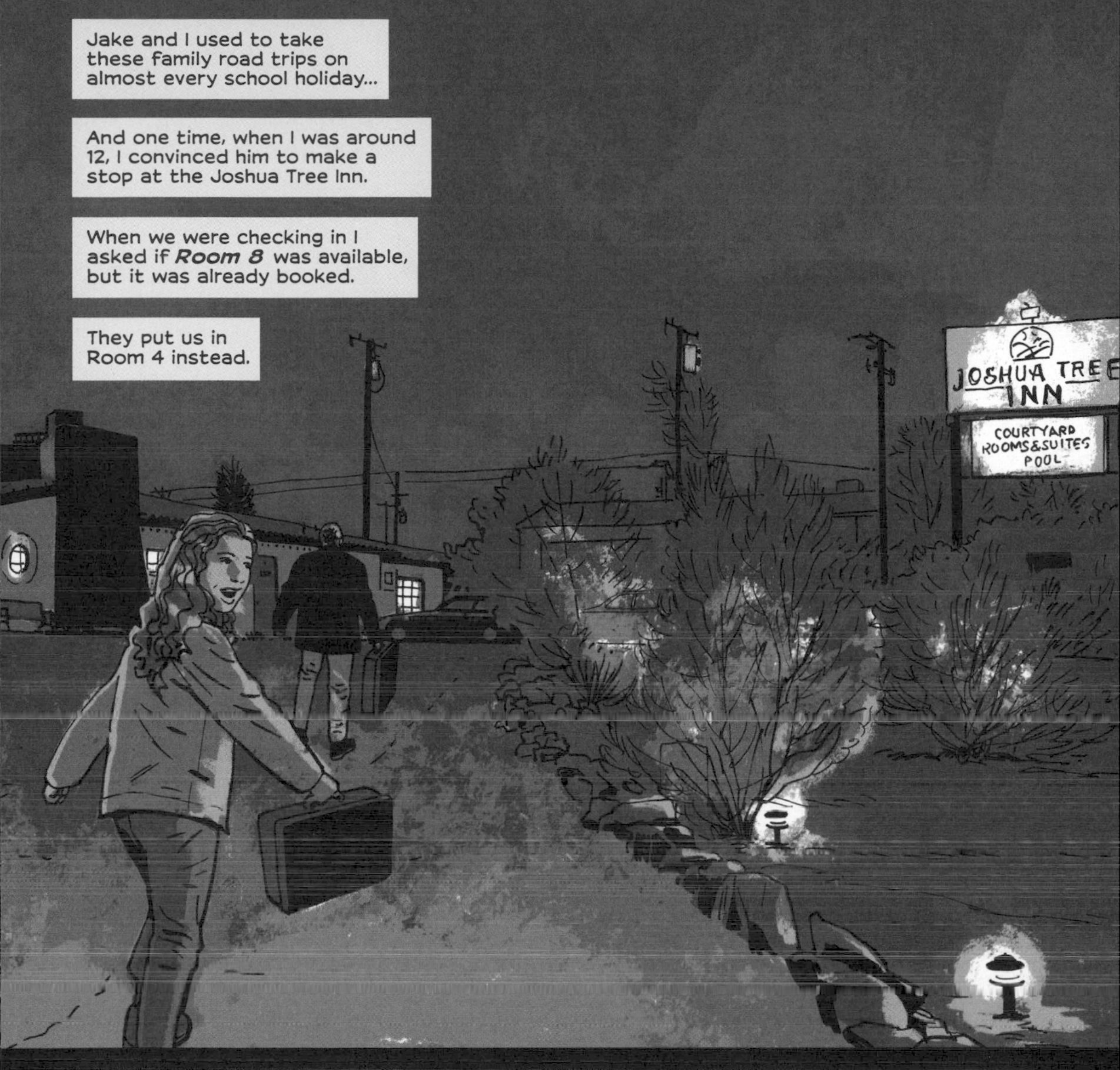
Jake and I used to take these family road trips on almost every school holiday...
And one time, when I was around 12, I convinced him to make a stop at the Joshua Tree Inn.
When we were checking in I asked if *Room 8* was available, but it was already booked.
They put us in Room 4 instead.
JOSHUA TREE INN
COURTYARD
ROOMS&SUITES
POOL

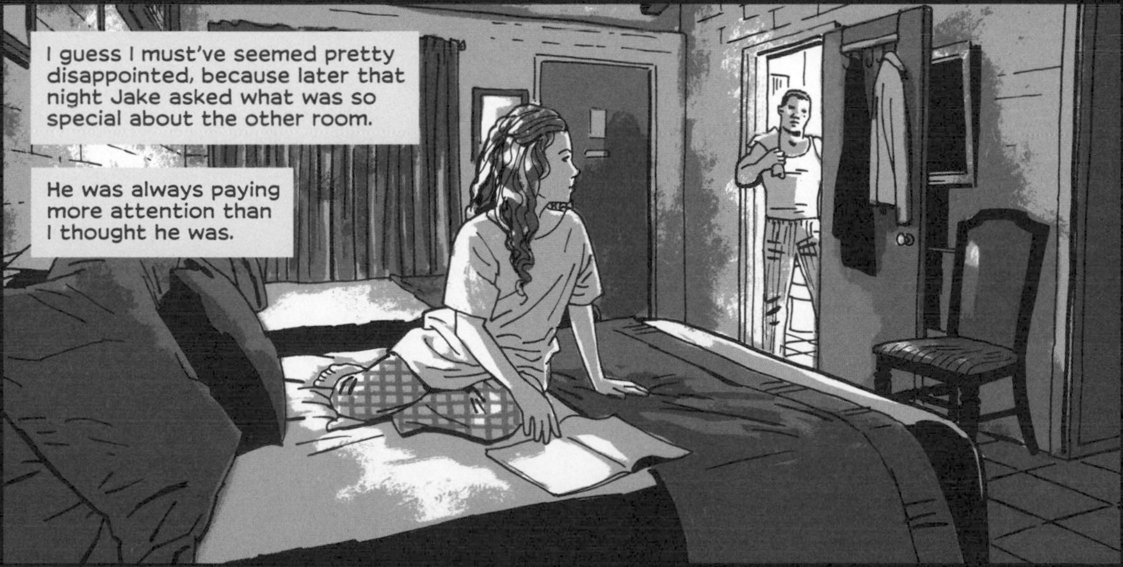
I guess I must've seemed pretty disappointed, because later that night Jake asked what was so special about the other room.
He was always paying more attention than I thought he was.

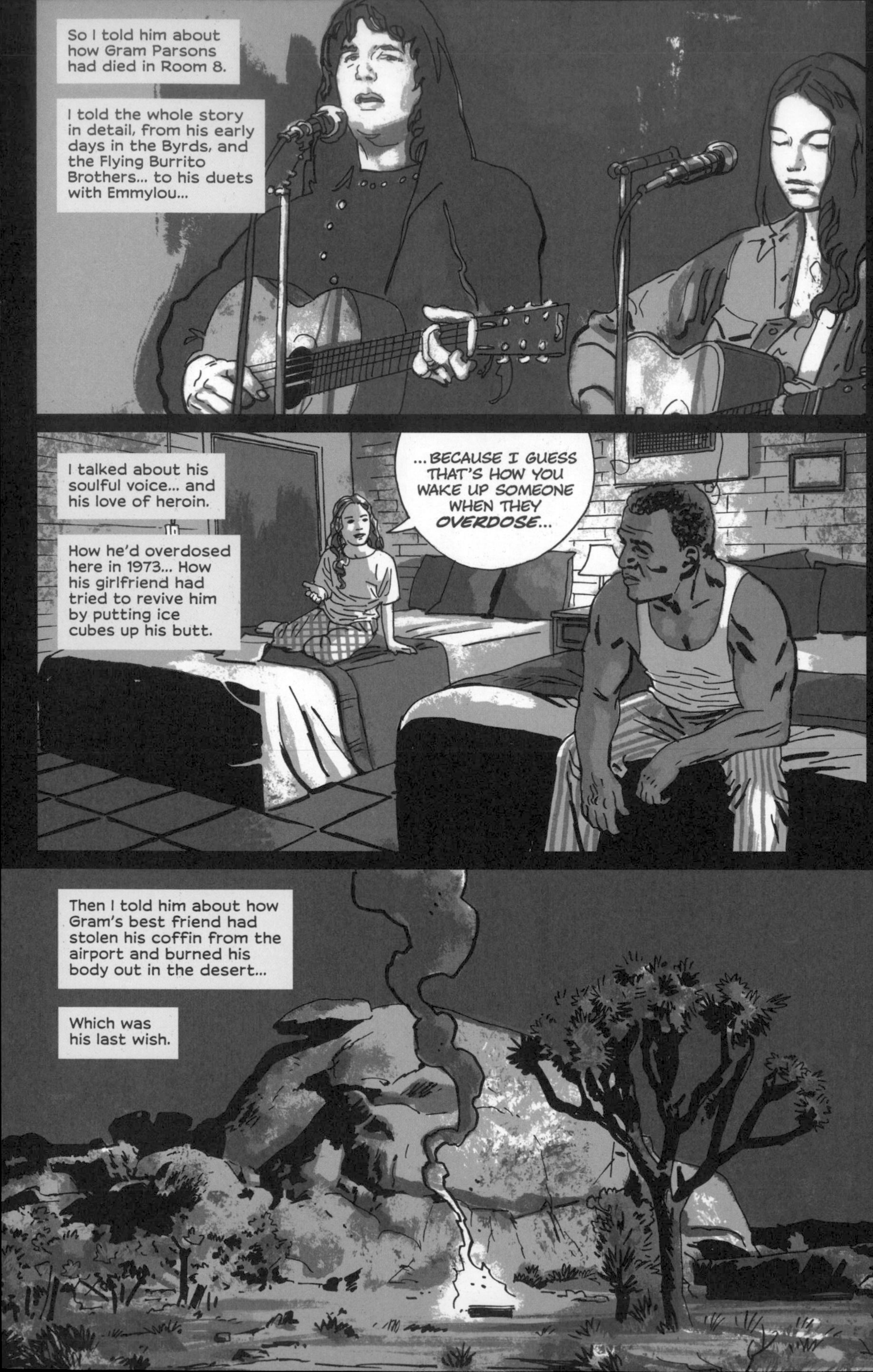
So I told him about how Gram Parsons had died in Room 8.
I told the whole story in detail, from his early days in the Byrds, and the Flying Burrito Brothers... to his duets with Emmylou...
I talked about his soulful voice... and his love of heroin.
How he'd overdosed here in 1973... How his girlfriend had tried to revive him by putting ice cubes up his butt.
...BECAUSE I GUESS THAT'S HOW YOU WAKE UP SOMEONE WHEN THEY *OVERDOSE*...
Then I told him about how Gram's best friend had stolen his coffin from the airport and burned his body out in the desert...
Which was his last wish.

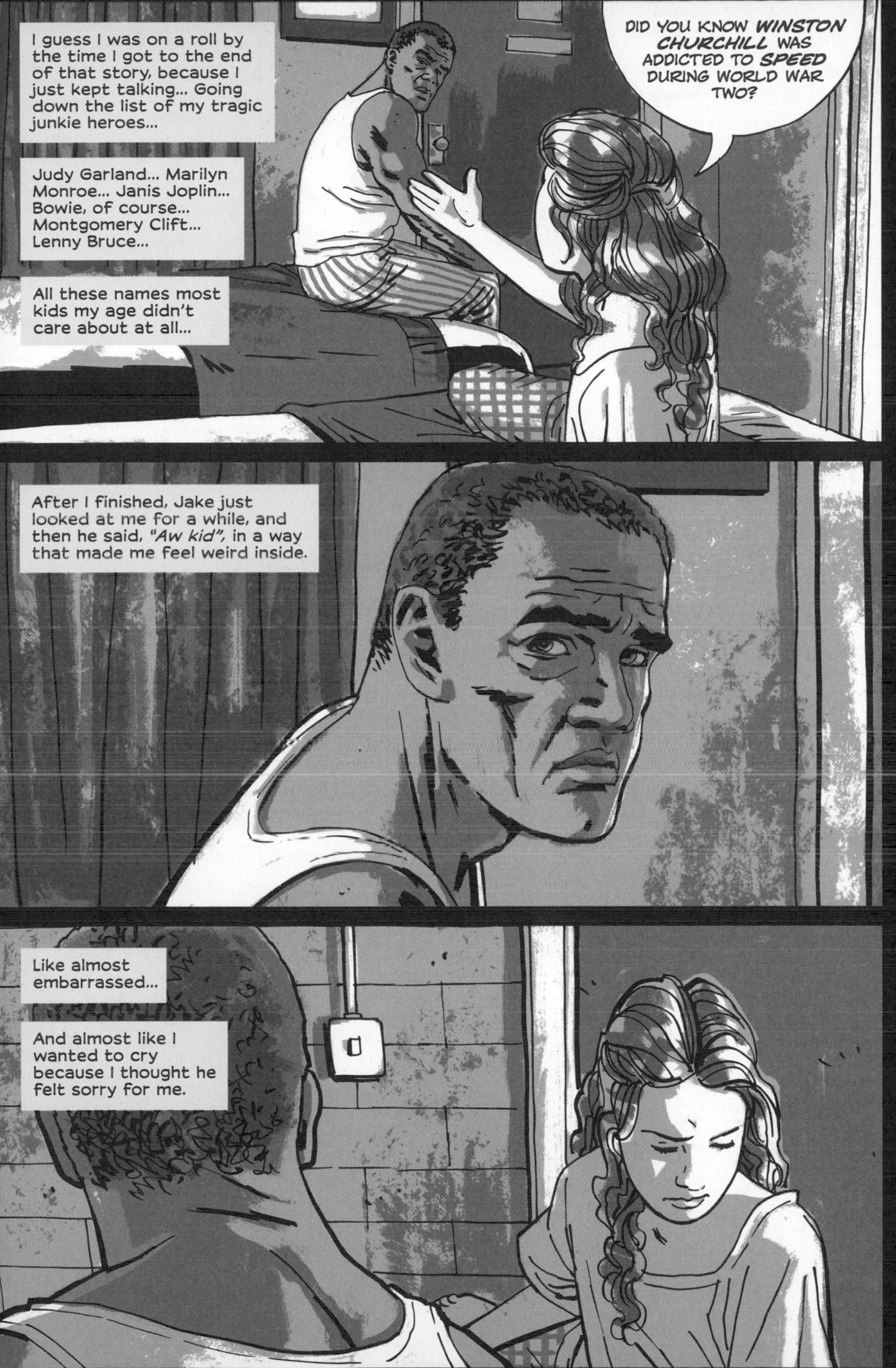
I guess I was on a roll by the time I got to the end of that story, because I just kept talking... Going down the list of my tragic junkie heroes...
DID YOU KNOW *WINSTON CHURCHILL* WAS ADDICTED TO *SPEED* DURING WORLD WAR TWO?
Judy Garland... Marilyn Monroe... Janis Joplin... Bowie, of course... Montgomery Clift... Lenny Bruce...
All these names most kids my age didn't care about at all...
After I finished, Jake just looked at me for a while, and then he said, *"Aw kid"*, in a way that made me feel weird inside.
Like almost embarrassed...
And almost like I wanted to cry because I thought he felt sorry for me.

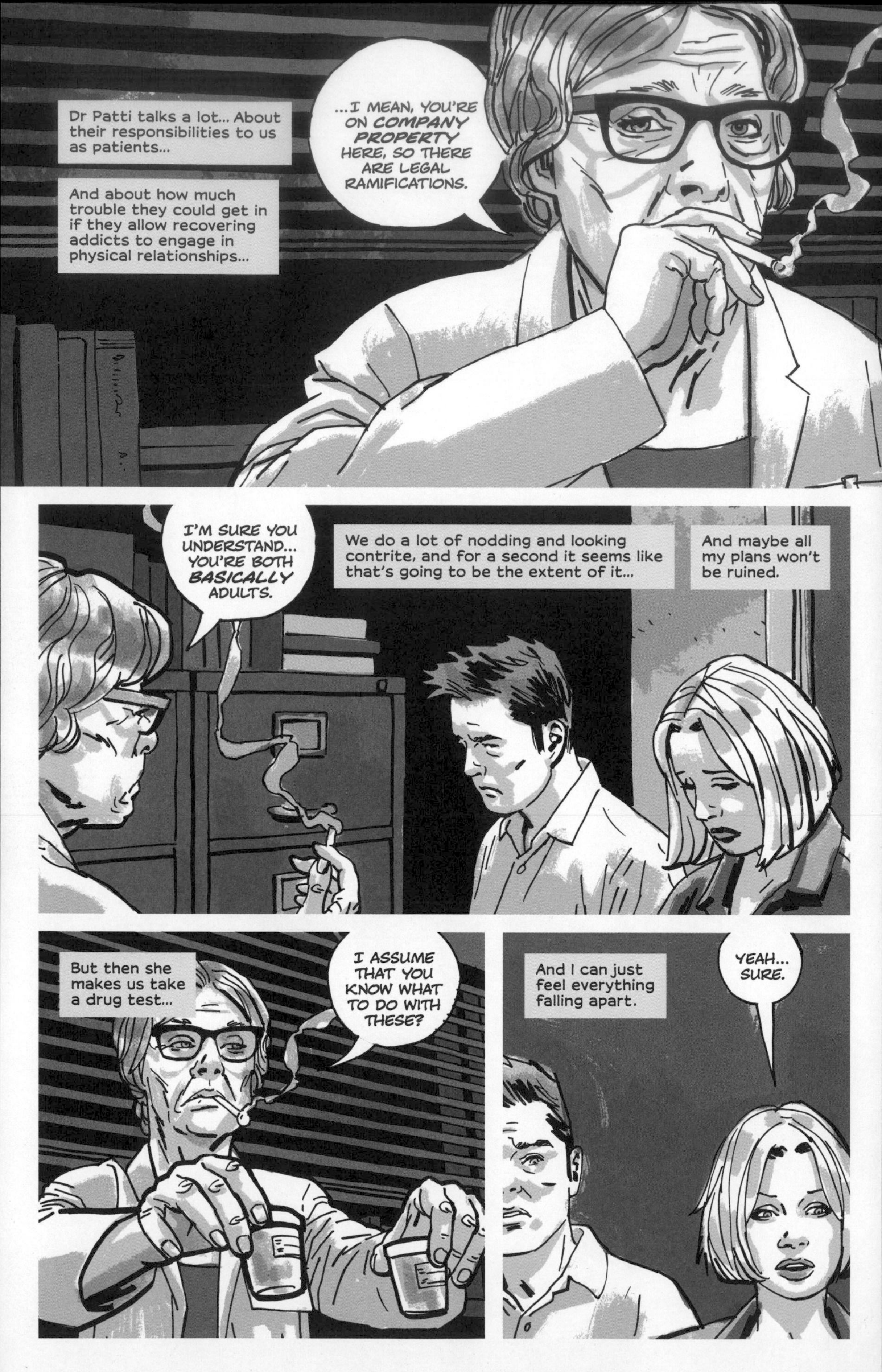
Dr Patti talks a lot... About their responsibilities to us as patients...
And about how much trouble they could get in if they allow recovering addicts to engage in physical relationships...
...I MEAN, YOU'RE ON COMPANY PROPERTY HERE, SO THERE ARE LEGAL RAMIFICATIONS.
I'M SURE YOU UNDERSTAND... YOU'RE BOTH BASICALLY ADULTS.
We do a lot of nodding and looking contrite, and for a second it seems like that's going to be the extent of it...
And maybe all my plans won't be ruined.
But then she makes us take a drug test...
I ASSUME THAT YOU KNOW WHAT TO DO WITH THESE?
And I can just feel everything falling apart.
YEAH... SURE.

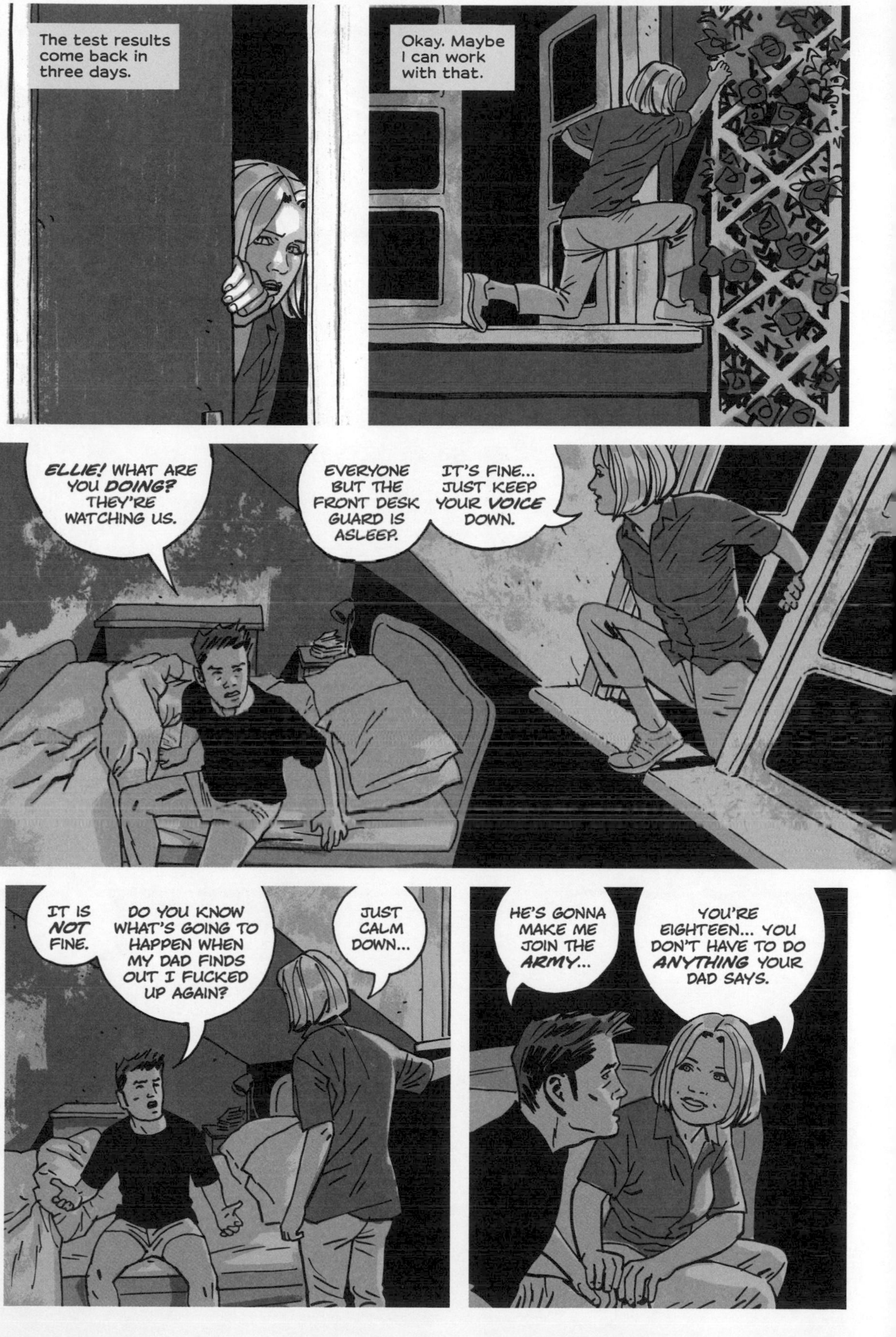

The test results come back in three days.
Okay. Maybe I can work with that.
ELLIE! WHAT ARE YOU DOING? THEY'RE WATCHING US.
EVERYONE BUT THE FRONT DESK GUARD IS ASLEEP.
IT'S FINE... JUST KEEP YOUR VOICE DOWN.
IT IS NOT FINE.
DO YOU KNOW WHAT'S GOING TO HAPPEN WHEN MY DAD FINDS OUT I FUCKED UP AGAIN?
JUST CALM DOWN...
HE'S GONNA MAKE ME JOIN THE ARMY...
YOU'RE EIGHTEEN... YOU DON'T HAVE TO DO ANYTHING YOUR DAD SAYS.

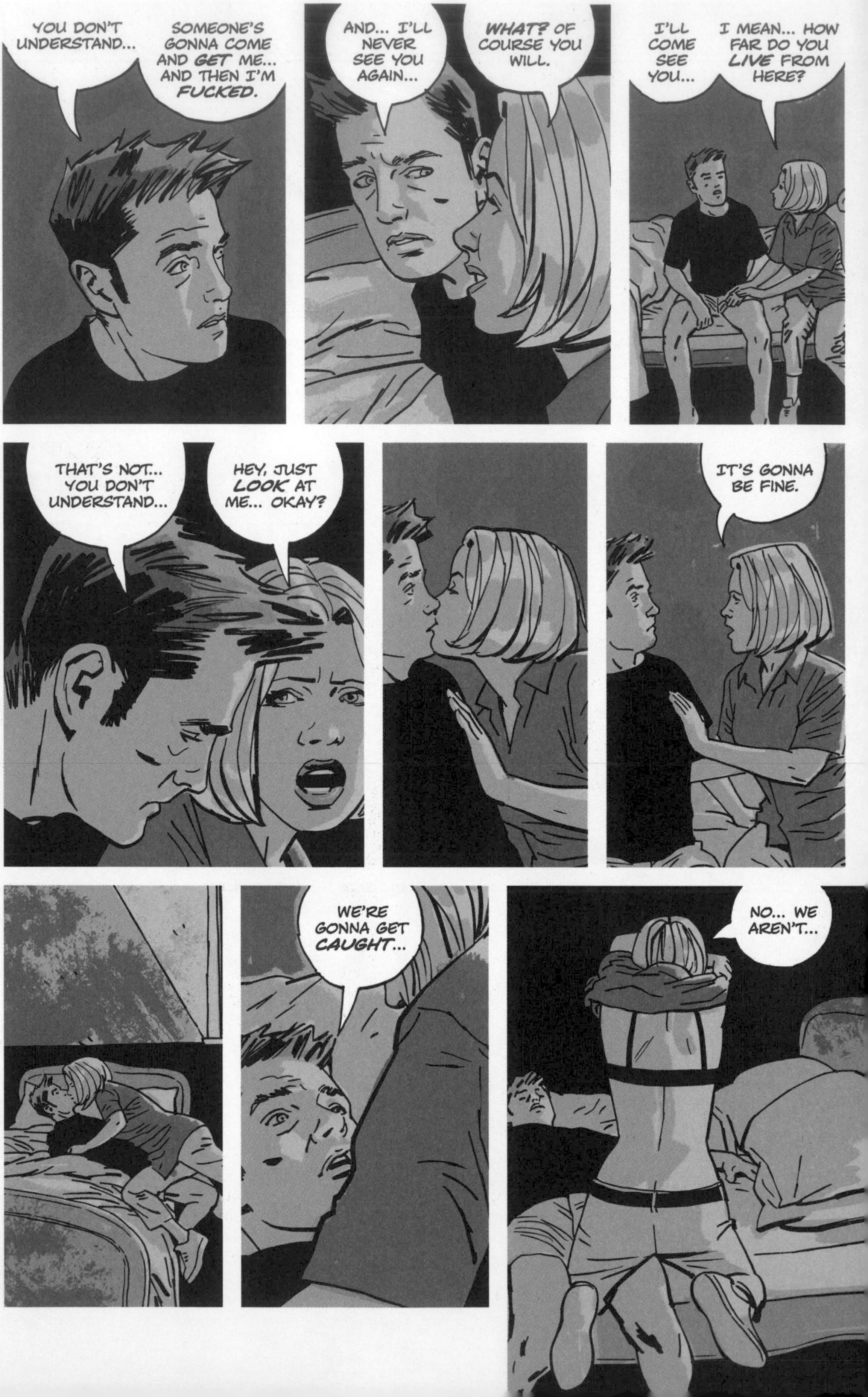
YOU DON'T UNDERSTAND...
SOMEONE'S GONNA COME AND GET ME... AND THEN I'M FUCKED.
AND... I'LL NEVER SEE YOU AGAIN...
WHAT? OF COURSE YOU WILL.
I'LL COME SEE YOU...
I MEAN... HOW FAR DO YOU LIVE FROM HERE?
THAT'S NOT... YOU DON'T UNDERSTAND...
HEY, JUST LOOK AT ME... OKAY?
IT'S GONNA BE FINE.
WE'RE GONNA GET CAUGHT...
NO... WE AREN'T...

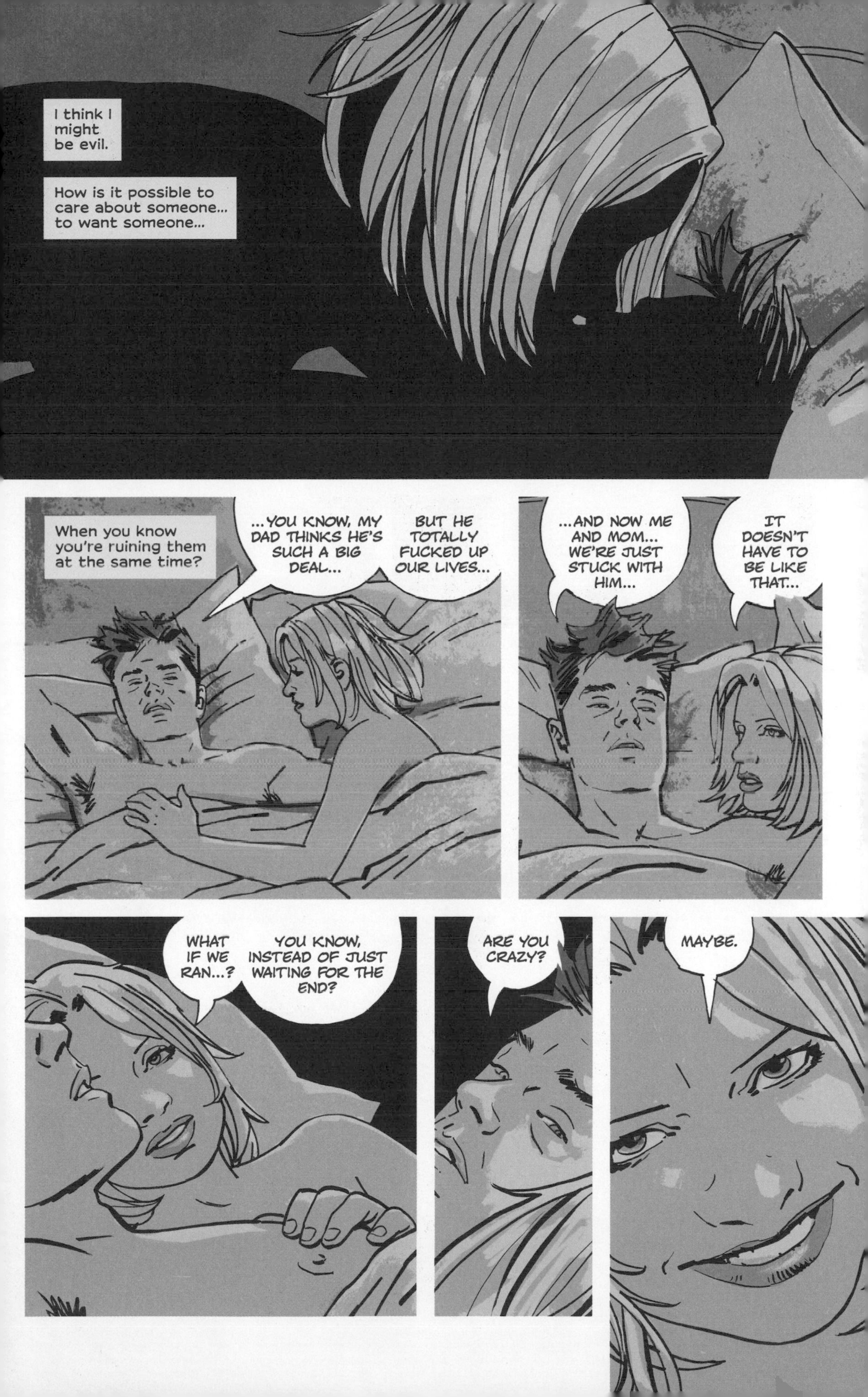
I think I might be evil.
How is it possible to care about someone... to want someone...
When you know you're ruining them at the same time?
...YOU KNOW, MY DAD THINKS HE'S SUCH A BIG DEAL...
BUT HE TOTALLY FUCKED UP OUR LIVES...
...AND NOW ME AND MOM... WE'RE JUST STUCK WITH HIM...
IT DOESN'T HAVE TO BE LIKE THAT...
WHAT IF WE RAN...?
YOU KNOW, INSTEAD OF JUST WAITING FOR THE END?
ARE YOU CRAZY?
MAYBE.

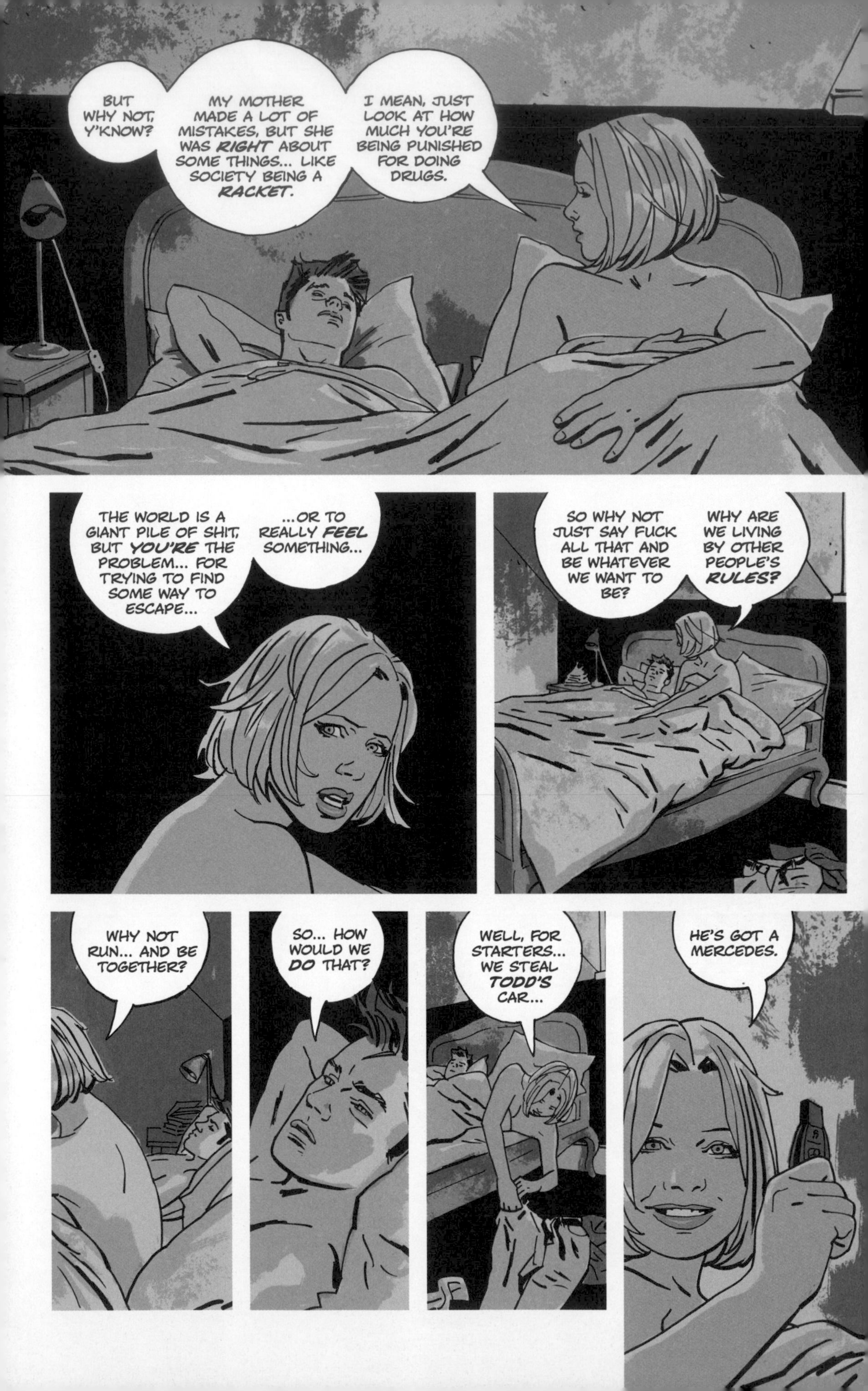
BUT WHY NOT, Y'KNOW?
MY MOTHER MADE A LOT OF MISTAKES, BUT SHE WAS RIGHT ABOUT SOME THINGS... LIKE SOCIETY BEING A RACKET.
I MEAN, JUST LOOK AT HOW MUCH YOU'RE BEING PUNISHED FOR DOING DRUGS.
THE WORLD IS A GIANT PILE OF SHIT, BUT YOU'RE THE PROBLEM... FOR TRYING TO FIND SOME WAY TO ESCAPE...
...OR TO REALLY FEEL SOMETHING...
SO WHY NOT JUST SAY FUCK ALL THAT AND BE WHATEVER WE WANT TO BE?
WHY ARE WE LIVING BY OTHER PEOPLE'S RULES?
WHY NOT RUN... AND BE TOGETHER?
SO... HOW WOULD WE DO THAT?
WELL, FOR STARTERS... WE STEAL TODD'S CAR...
HE'S GOT A MERCEDES.

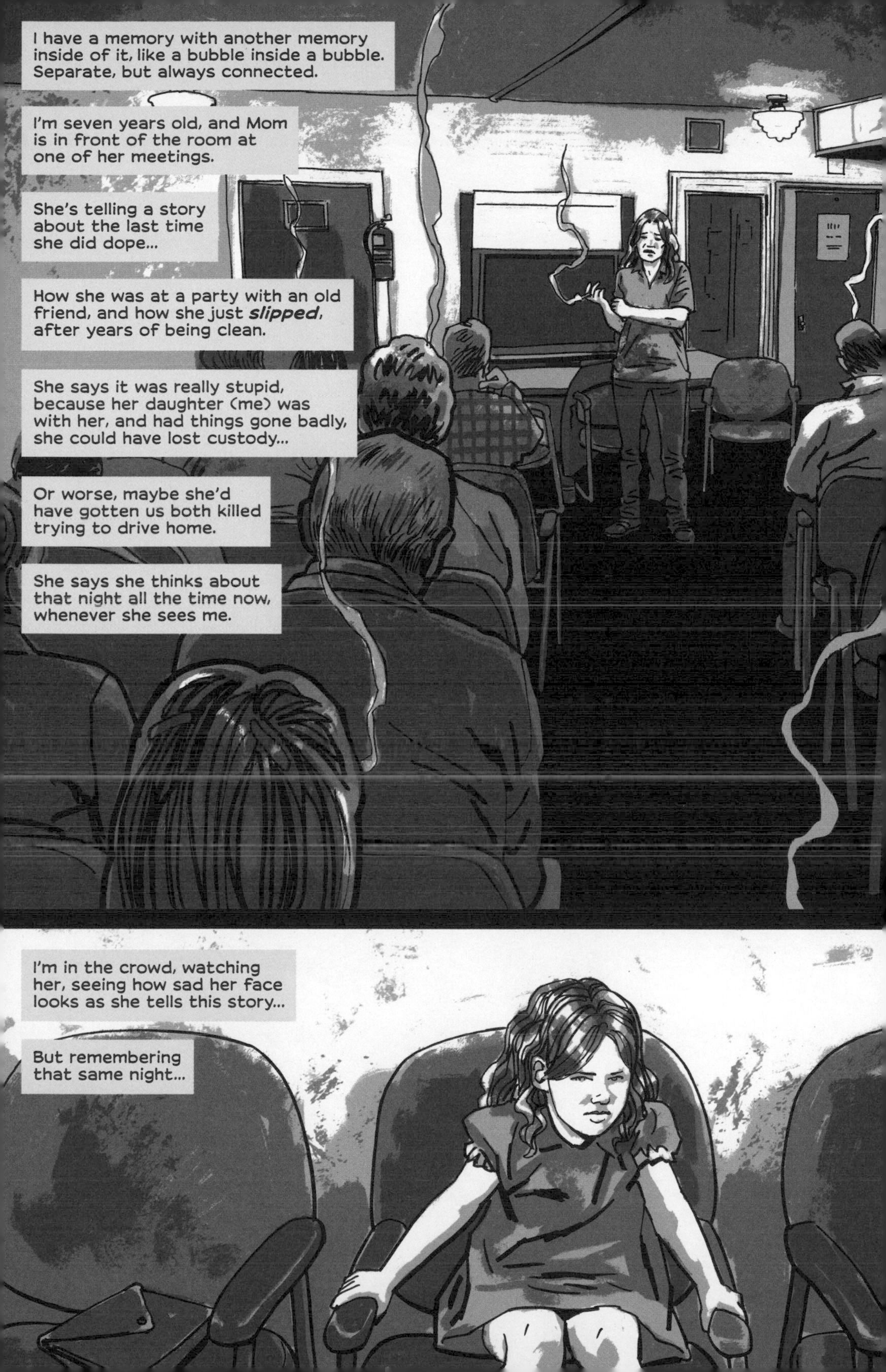
I have a memory with another memory inside of it, like a bubble inside a bubble. Separate, but always connected.
I'm seven years old, and Mom is in front of the room at one of her meetings.
She's telling a story about the last time she did dope...
How she was at a party with an old friend, and how she just *slipped*, after years of being clean.
She says it was really stupid, because her daughter (me) was with her, and had things gone badly, she could have lost custody...
Or worse, maybe she'd have gotten us both killed trying to drive home.
She says she thinks about that night all the time now, whenever she sees me.
I'm in the crowd, watching her, seeing how sad her face looks as she tells this story...
But remembering that same night...

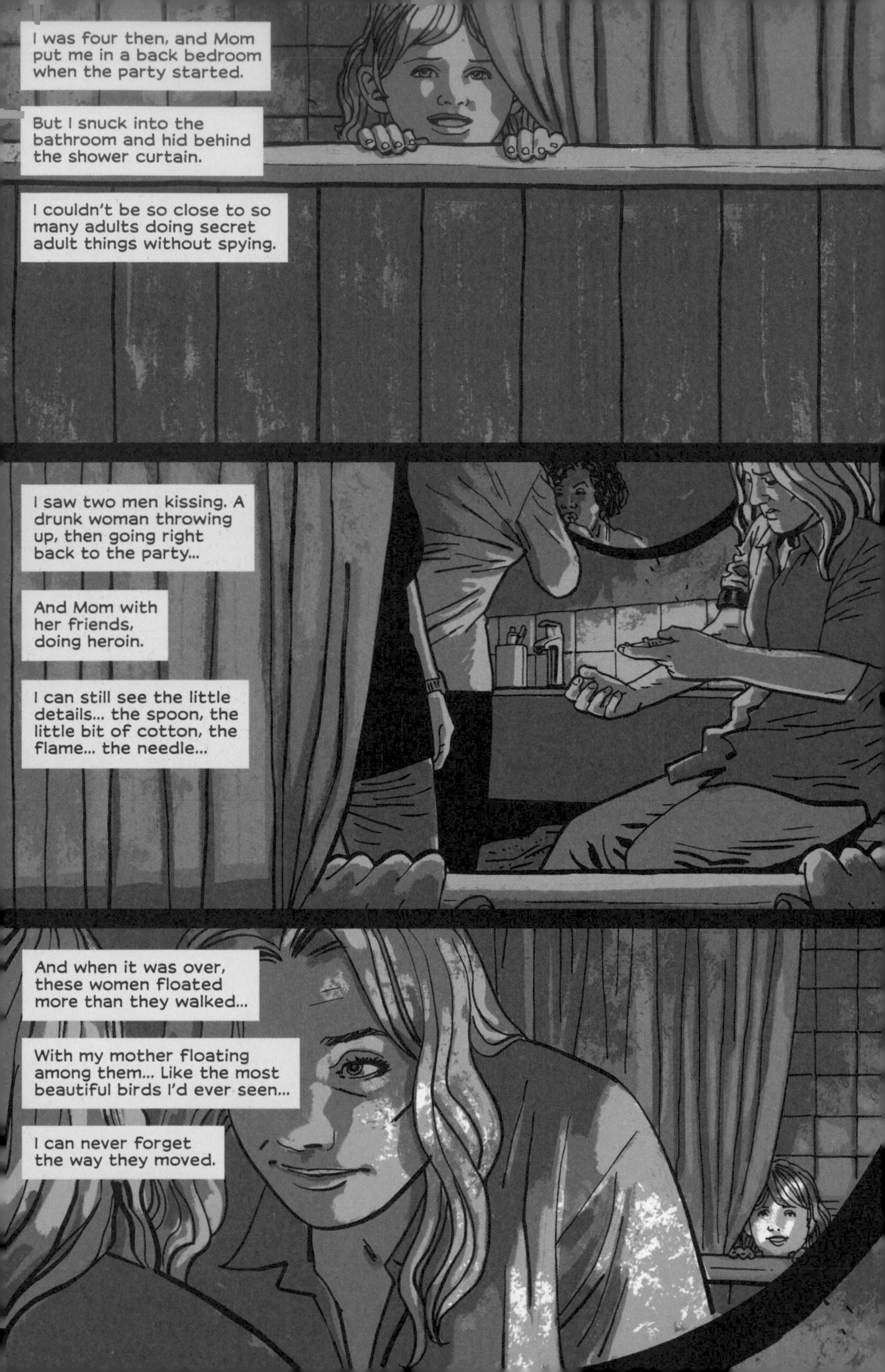
I was four then, and Mom put me in a back bedroom when the party started.
But I snuck into the bathroom and hid behind the shower curtain.
I couldn't be so close to so many adults doing secret adult things without spying.
I saw two men kissing. A drunk woman throwing up, then going right back to the party...
And Mom with her friends, doing heroin.
I can still see the little details... the spoon, the little bit of cotton, the flame... the needle...
And when it was over, these women floated more than they walked...
With my mother floating among them... Like the most beautiful birds I'd ever seen...
I can never forget the way they moved.

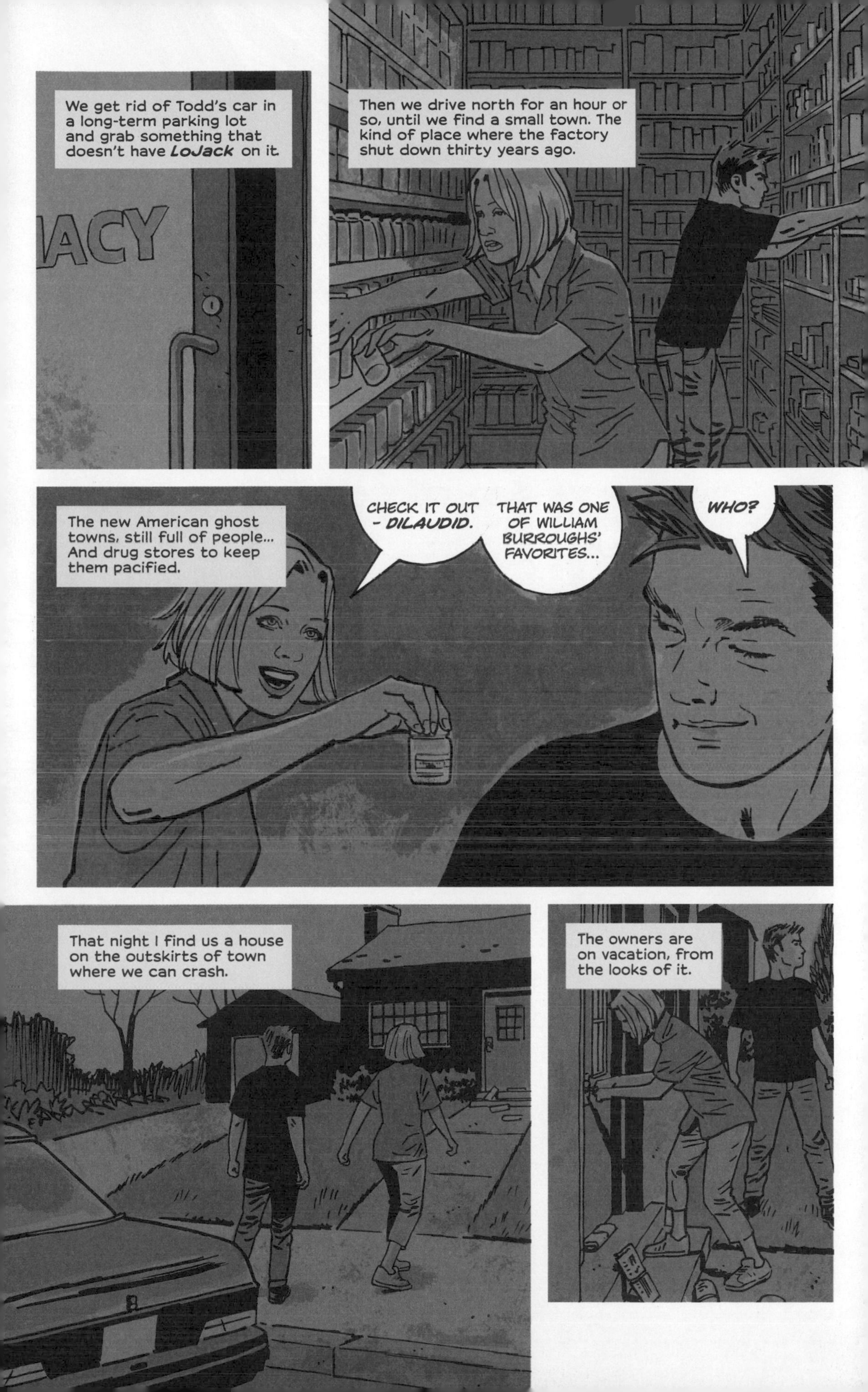

We get rid of Todd's car in a long-term parking lot and grab something that doesn't have *LoJack* on it.
ACY
Then we drive north for an hour or so, until we find a small town. The kind of place where the factory shut down thirty years ago.
The new American ghost towns, still full of people... And drug stores to keep them pacified.
CHECK IT OUT - *DILAUDID*.
THAT WAS ONE OF WILLIAM BURROUGHS' FAVORITES...
WHO?
That night I find us a house on the outskirts of town where we can crash.
The owners are on vacation, from the looks of it.

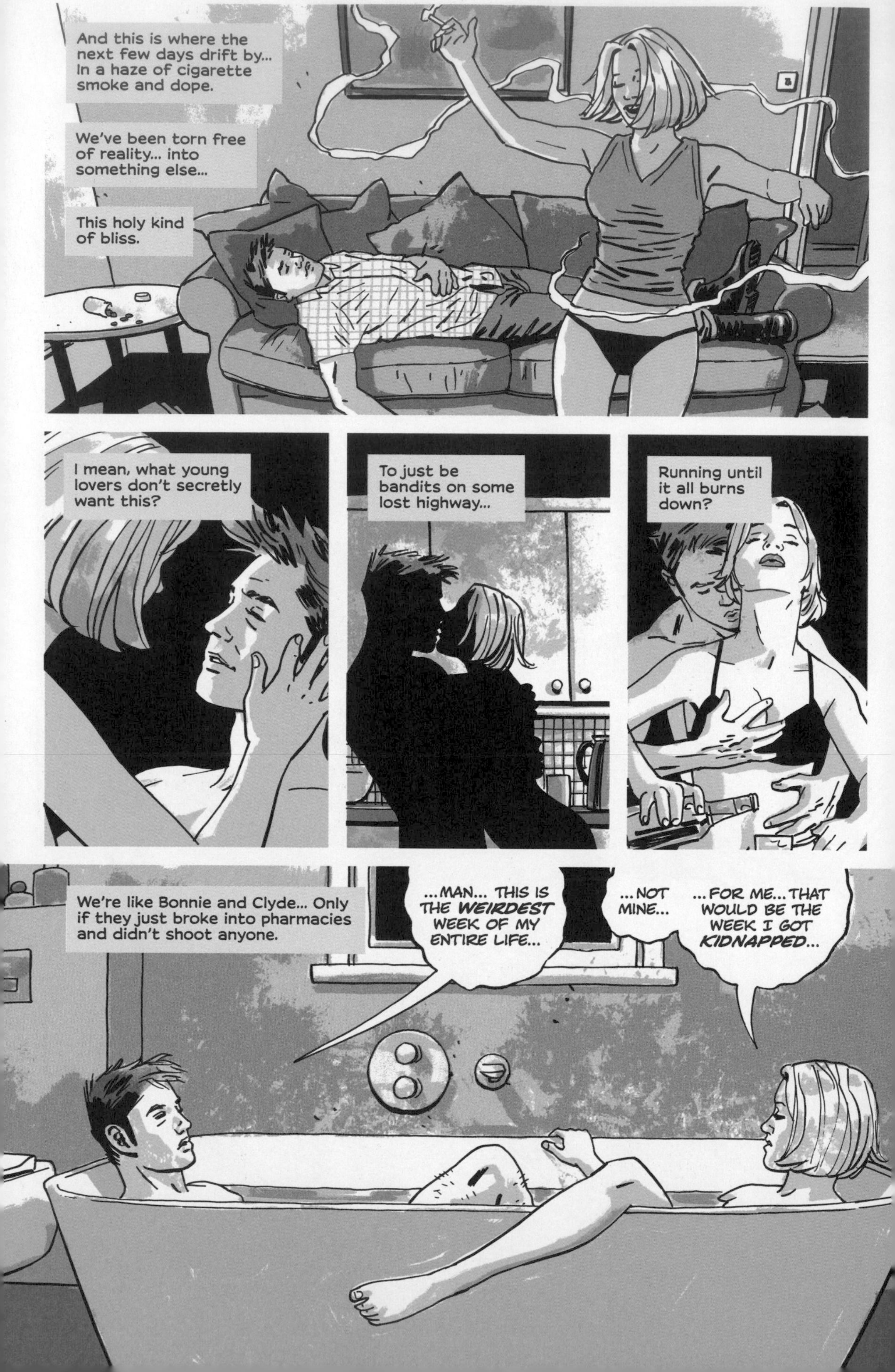
And this is where the next few days drift by... In a haze of cigarette smoke and dope.
We've been torn free of reality... into something else...
This holy kind of bliss.
I mean, what young lovers don't secretly want this?
To just be bandits on some lost highway...
Running until it all burns down?
We're like Bonnie and Clyde... Only if they just broke into pharmacies and didn't shoot anyone.
...MAN... THIS IS THE *WEIRDEST* WEEK OF MY ENTIRE LIFE...
...NOT MINE...
...FOR ME... THAT WOULD BE THE WEEK I GOT *KIDNAPPED*...

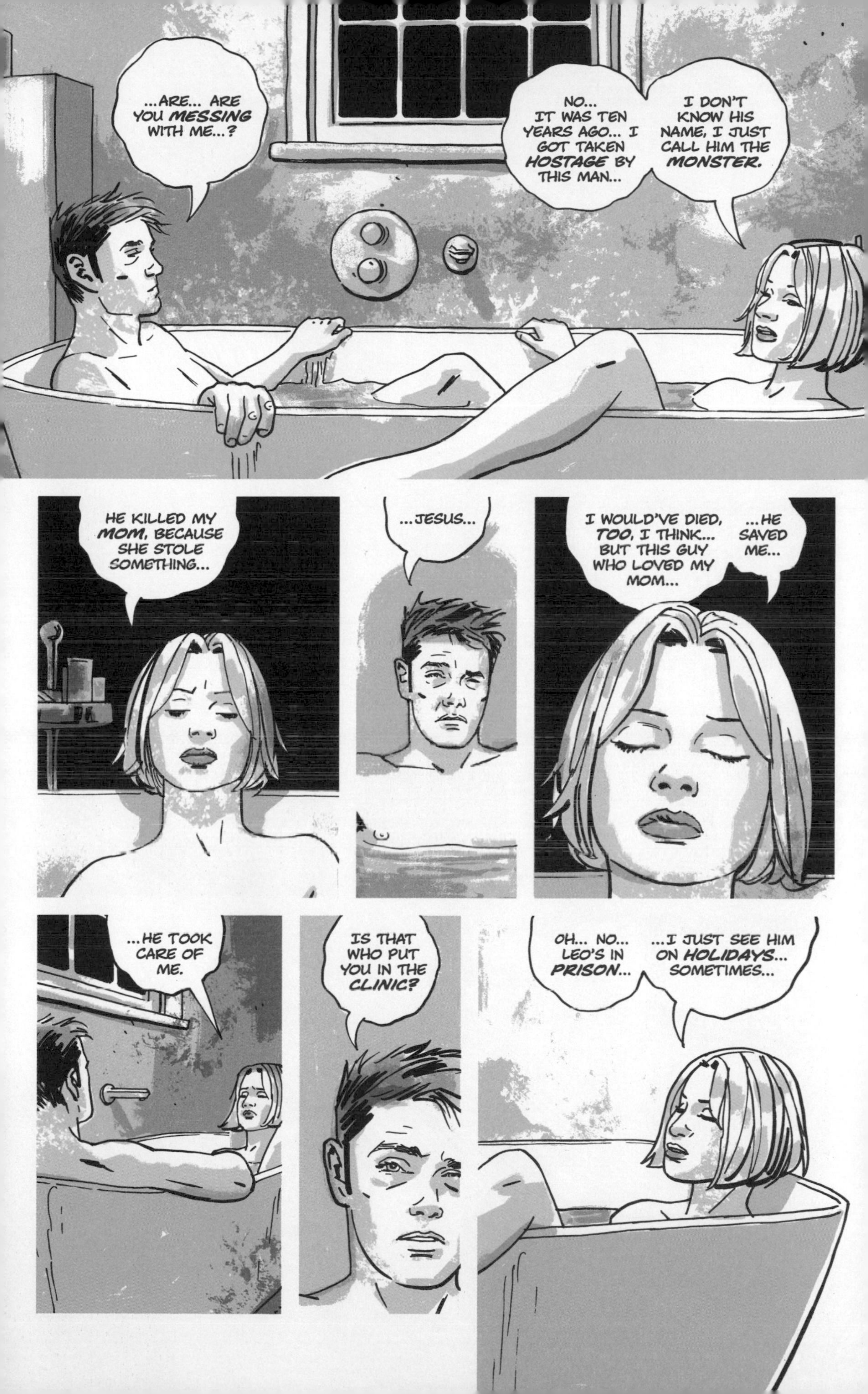
...ARE... ARE YOU MESSING WITH ME...?
NO... IT WAS TEN YEARS AGO... I GOT TAKEN HOSTAGE BY THIS MAN...
I DON'T KNOW HIS NAME, I JUST CALL HIM THE MONSTER.
HE KILLED MY MOM, BECAUSE SHE STOLE SOMETHING...
...JESUS...
I WOULD'VE DIED, TOO, I THINK... BUT THIS GUY WHO LOVED MY MOM...
...HE SAVED ME...
...HE TOOK CARE OF ME.
IS THAT WHO PUT YOU IN THE CLINIC?
OH... NO... LEO'S IN PRISON...
...I JUST SEE HIM ON HOLIDAYS... SOMETIMES...

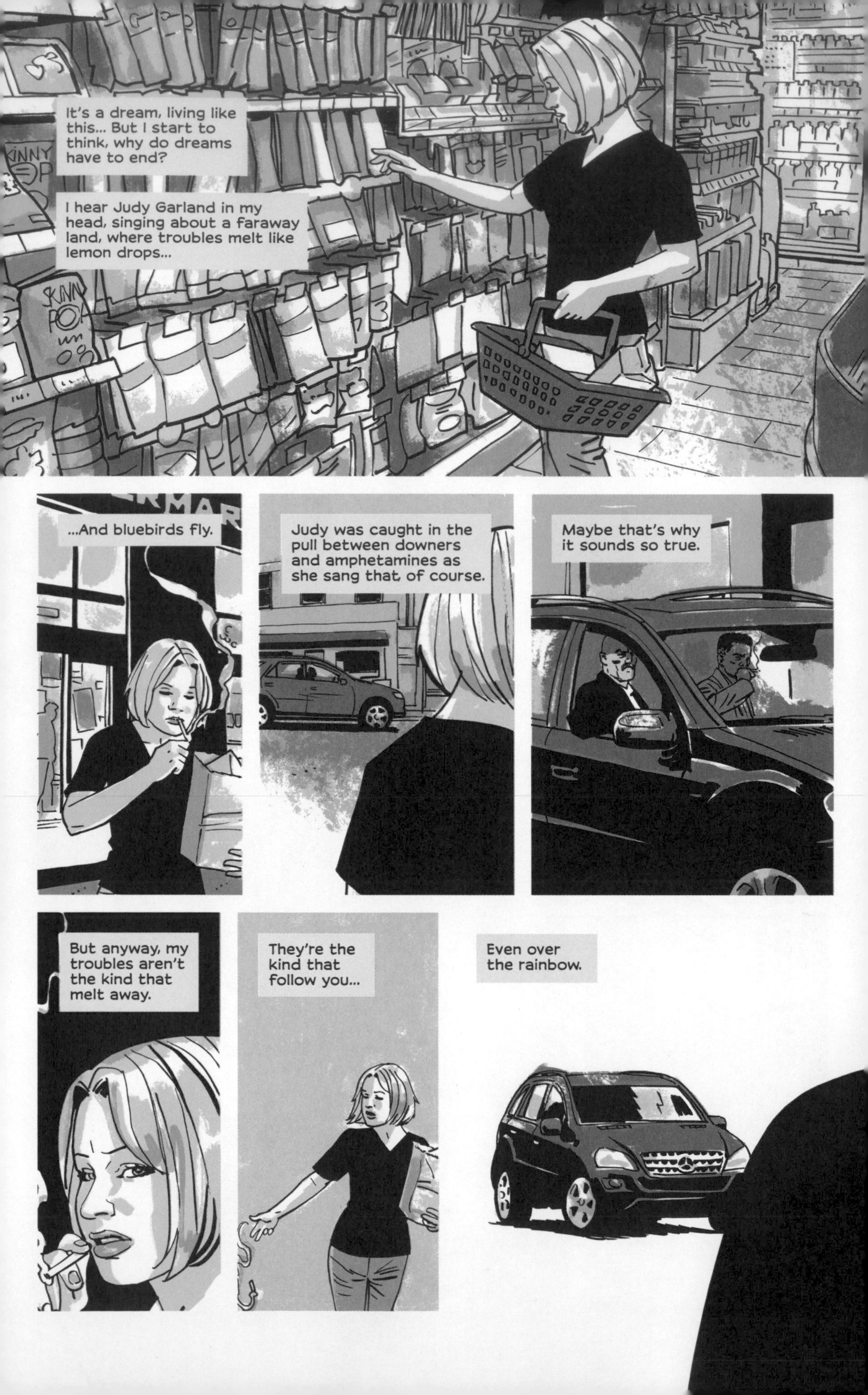
It's a dream, living like this... But I start to think, why do dreams have to end?
I hear Judy Garland in my head, singing about a faraway land, where troubles melt like lemon drops...
...And bluebirds fly.
Judy was caught in the pull between downers and amphetamines as she sang that, of course.
Maybe that's why it sounds so true.
But anyway, my troubles aren't the kind that melt away.
They're the kind that follow you...
Even over the rainbow.

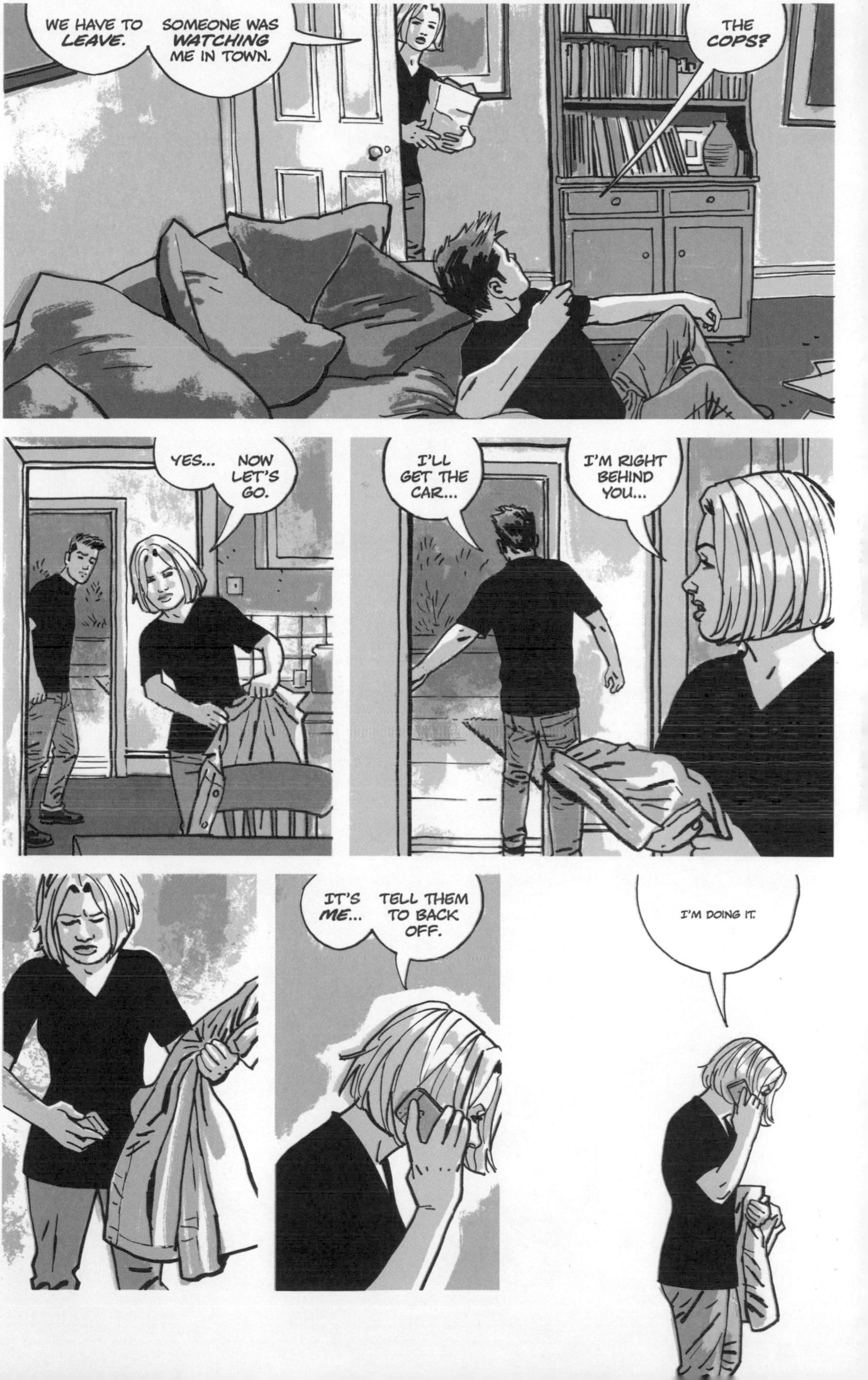
WE HAVE TO *LEAVE.*
SOMEONE WAS *WATCHING* ME IN TOWN.
THE *COPS?*
YES... NOW LET'S GO.
I'LL GET THE CAR...
I'M RIGHT BEHIND YOU...
IT'S *ME*... TELL THEM TO BACK OFF.
I'M DOING IT.

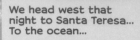

We head west that night to Santa Teresa... To the ocean...

Skip says the sky reminds him of a Van Gogh painting as we drive into it.

And I tell him that you have to be on drugs to really see the sky the way Van Gogh did...

Because he was addicted to absinthe and digitalis, which changed the way he saw color.

They made it more vibrant...

More alive.

Skip looks at the sky ahead like he wants to agree...

But he doesn't say anything. We just drive.

And I try to live inside that silence as long as it lasts.

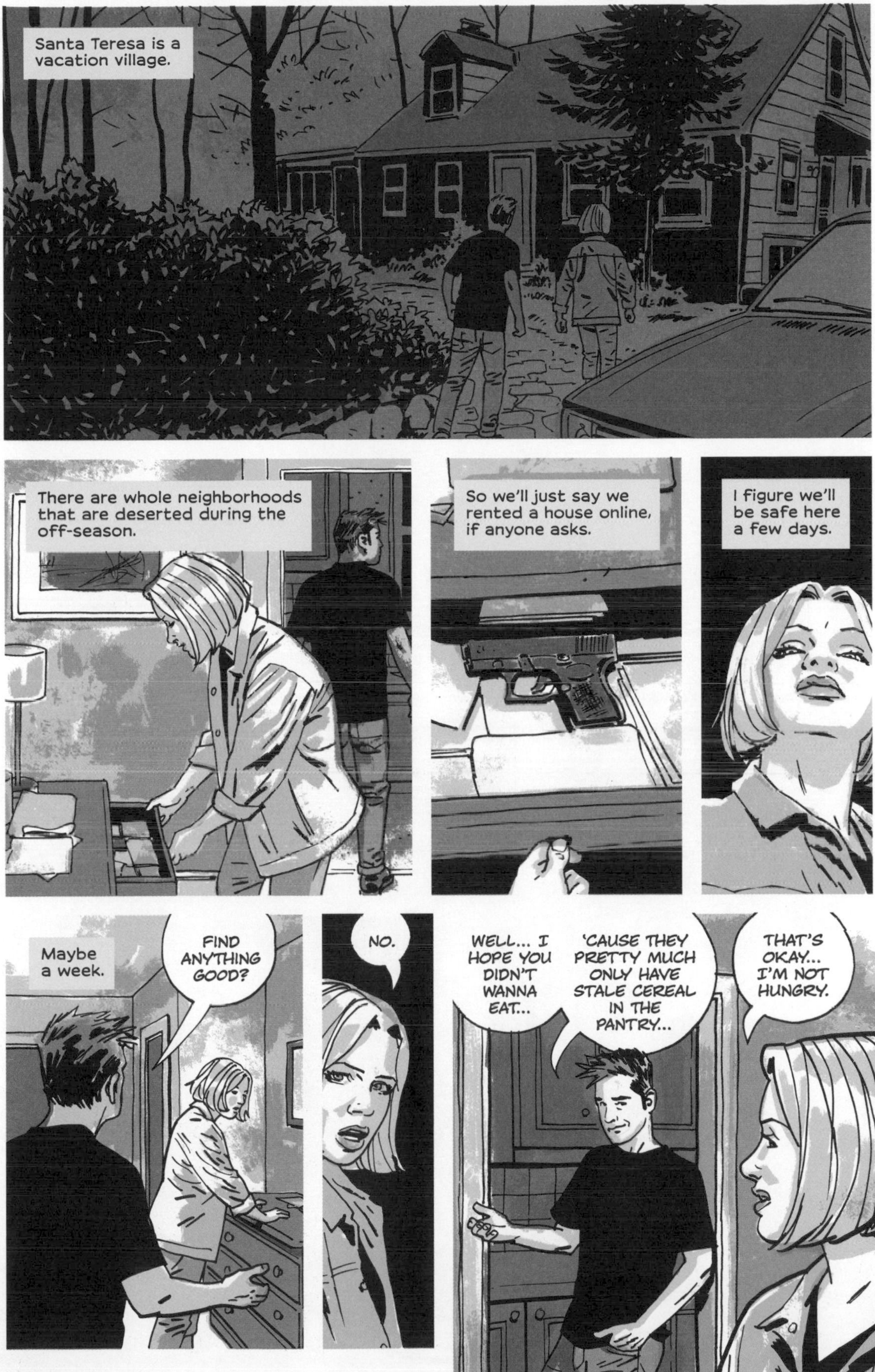
Santa Teresa is a vacation village.
There are whole neighborhoods that are deserted during the off-season.
So we'll just say we rented a house online, if anyone asks.
I figure we'll be safe here a few days.
Maybe a week.
FIND ANYTHING GOOD?
NO.
WELL... I HOPE YOU DIDN'T WANNA EAT...
'CAUSE THEY PRETTY MUCH ONLY HAVE STALE CEREAL IN THE PANTRY...
THAT'S OKAY... I'M NOT HUNGRY.

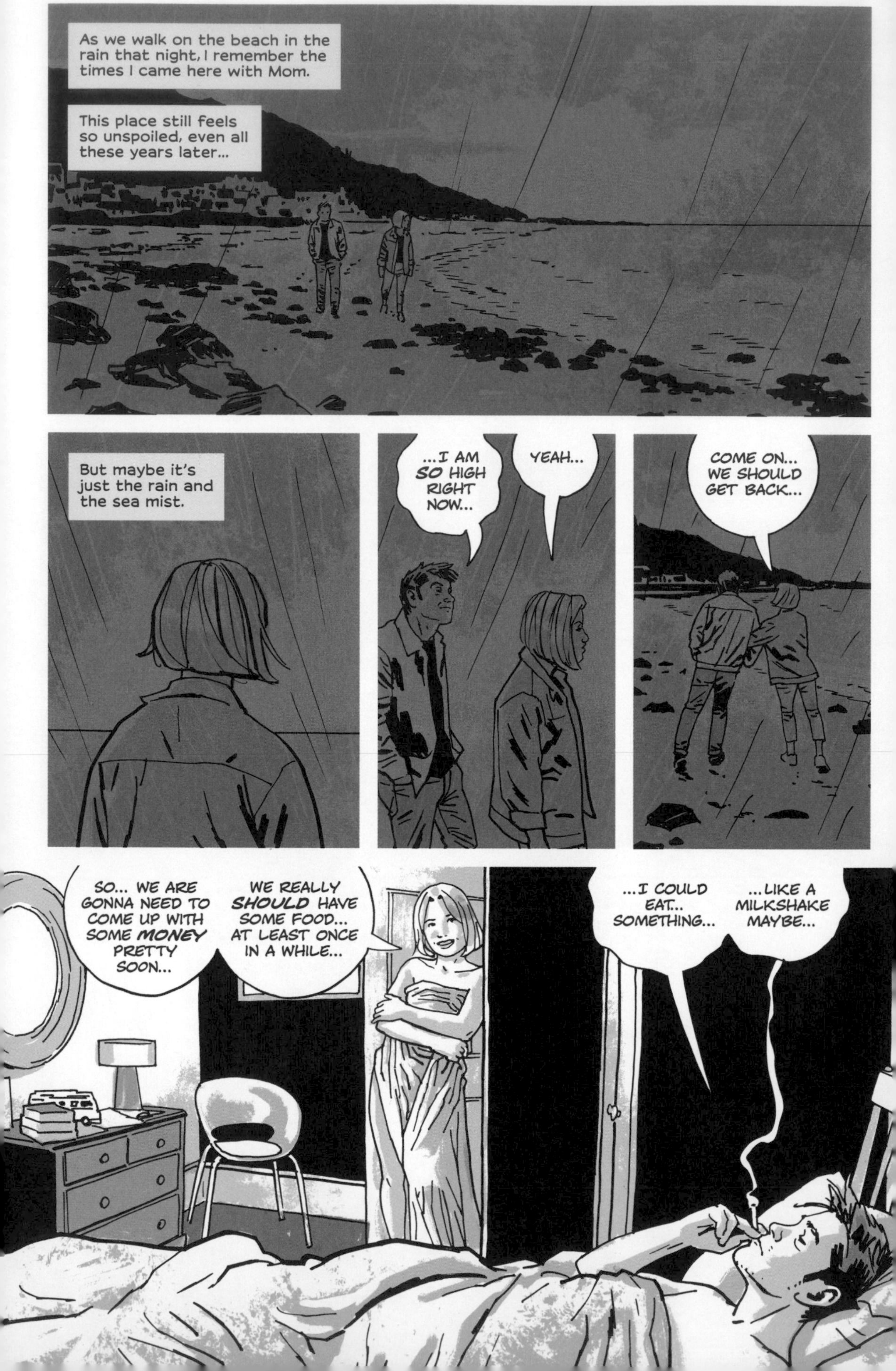
As we walk on the beach in the rain that night, I remember the times I came here with Mom.
This place still feels so unspoiled, even all these years later...
But maybe it's just the rain and the sea mist.
...I AM SO HIGH RIGHT NOW...
YEAH...
COME ON... WE SHOULD GET BACK...
SO... WE ARE GONNA NEED TO COME UP WITH SOME MONEY PRETTY SOON...
WE REALLY SHOULD HAVE SOME FOOD... AT LEAST ONCE IN A WHILE...
...I COULD EAT... SOMETHING...
...LIKE A MILKSHAKE MAYBE...

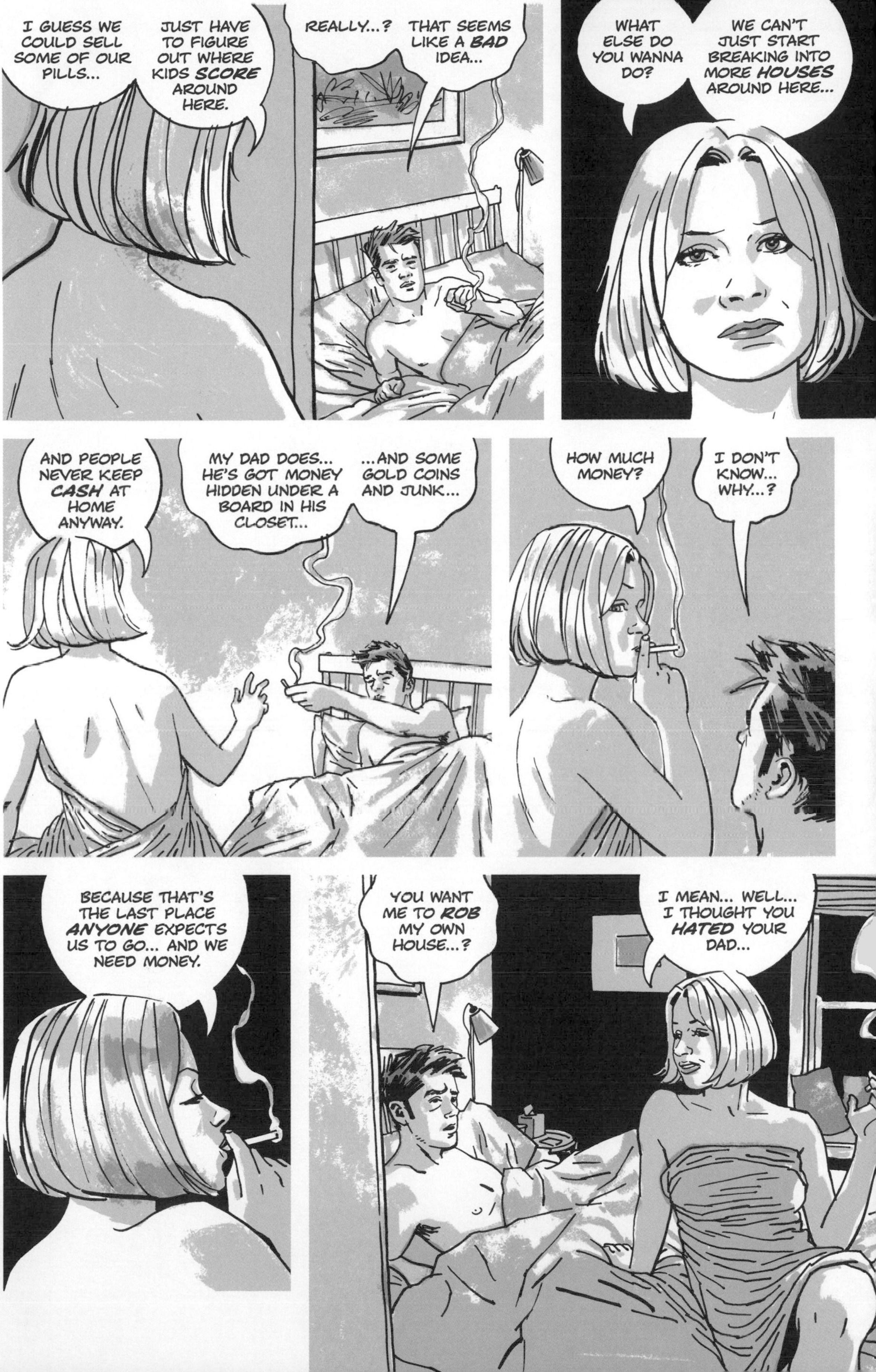
I GUESS WE COULD SELL SOME OF OUR PILLS...
JUST HAVE TO FIGURE OUT WHERE KIDS SCORE AROUND HERE.
REALLY...?
THAT SEEMS LIKE A BAD IDEA...
WHAT ELSE DO YOU WANNA DO?
WE CAN'T JUST START BREAKING INTO MORE HOUSES AROUND HERE...
AND PEOPLE NEVER KEEP CASH AT HOME ANYWAY.
MY DAD DOES... HE'S GOT MONEY HIDDEN UNDER A BOARD IN HIS CLOSET...
...AND SOME GOLD COINS AND JUNK...
HOW MUCH MONEY?
I DON'T KNOW... WHY...?
BECAUSE THAT'S THE LAST PLACE ANYONE EXPECTS US TO GO... AND WE NEED MONEY.
YOU WANT ME TO ROB MY OWN HOUSE...?
I MEAN... WELL... I THOUGHT YOU HATED YOUR DAD...

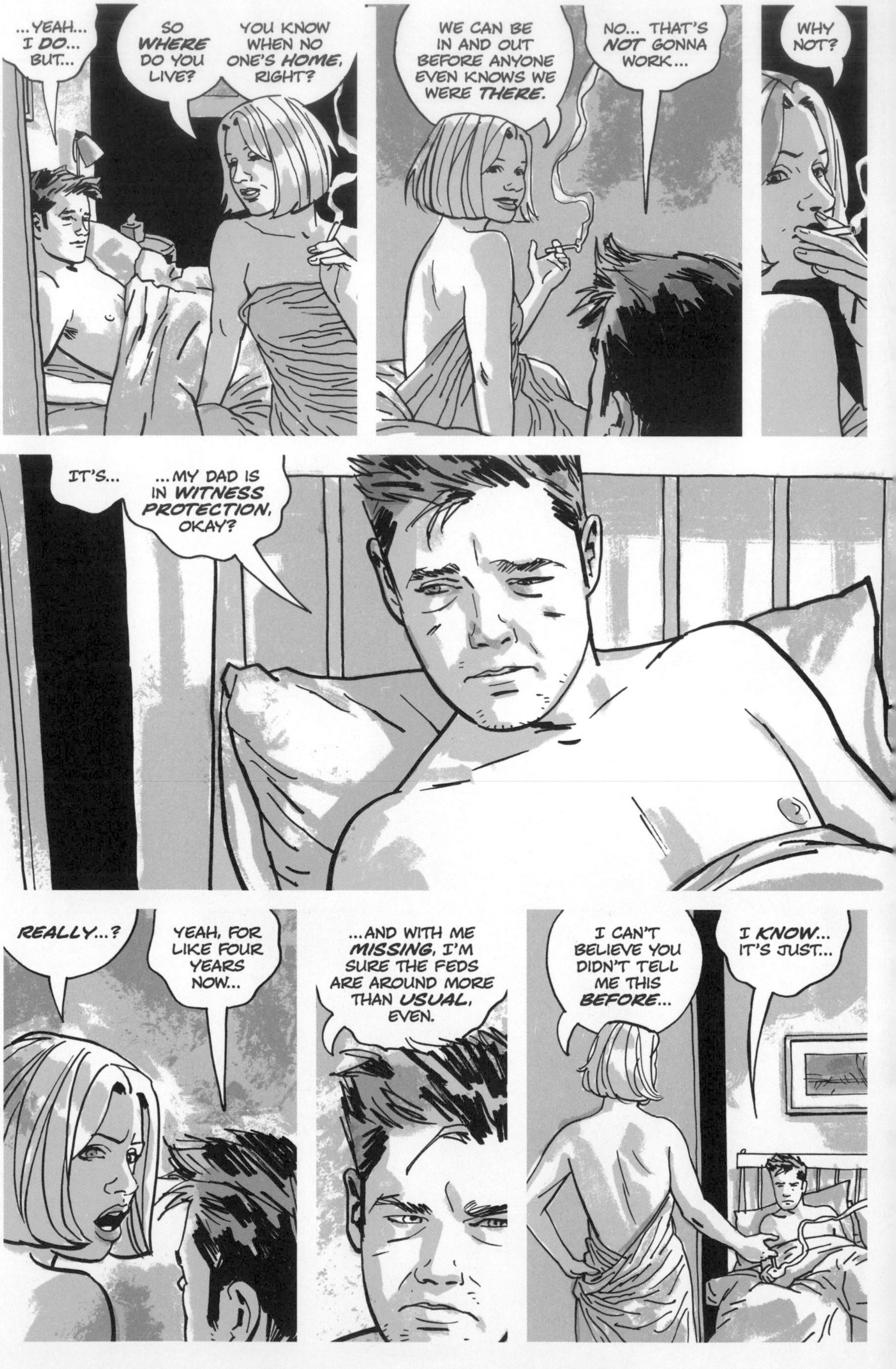
...YEAH... I DO... BUT...
SO WHERE DO YOU LIVE?
YOU KNOW WHEN NO ONE'S HOME, RIGHT?
WE CAN BE IN AND OUT BEFORE ANYONE EVEN KNOWS WE WERE THERE.
NO... THAT'S NOT GONNA WORK...
WHY NOT?
IT'S...
...MY DAD IS IN WITNESS PROTECTION, OKAY?
REALLY...?
YEAH, FOR LIKE FOUR YEARS NOW...
...AND WITH ME MISSING, I'M SURE THE FEDS ARE AROUND MORE THAN USUAL, EVEN.
I CAN'T BELIEVE YOU DIDN'T TELL ME THIS BEFORE...
I KNOW... IT'S JUST...

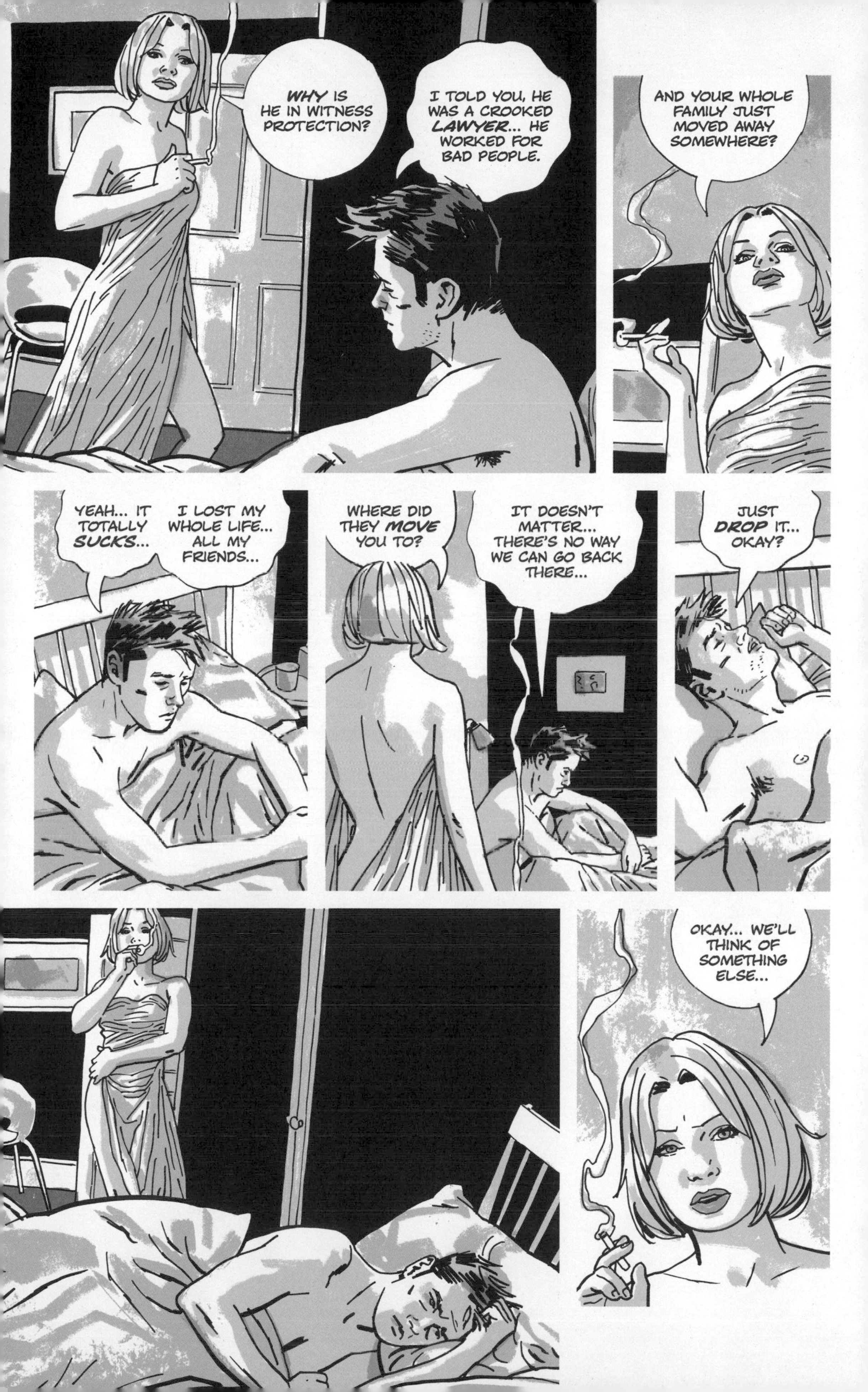
WHY IS HE IN WITNESS PROTECTION?
I TOLD YOU, HE WAS A CROOKED LAWYER... HE WORKED FOR BAD PEOPLE.
AND YOUR WHOLE FAMILY JUST MOVED AWAY SOMEWHERE?
YEAH... IT TOTALLY SUCKS...
I LOST MY WHOLE LIFE... ALL MY FRIENDS...
WHERE DID THEY MOVE YOU TO?
IT DOESN'T MATTER... THERE'S NO WAY WE CAN GO BACK THERE...
JUST DROP IT... OKAY?
OKAY... WE'LL THINK OF SOMETHING ELSE...

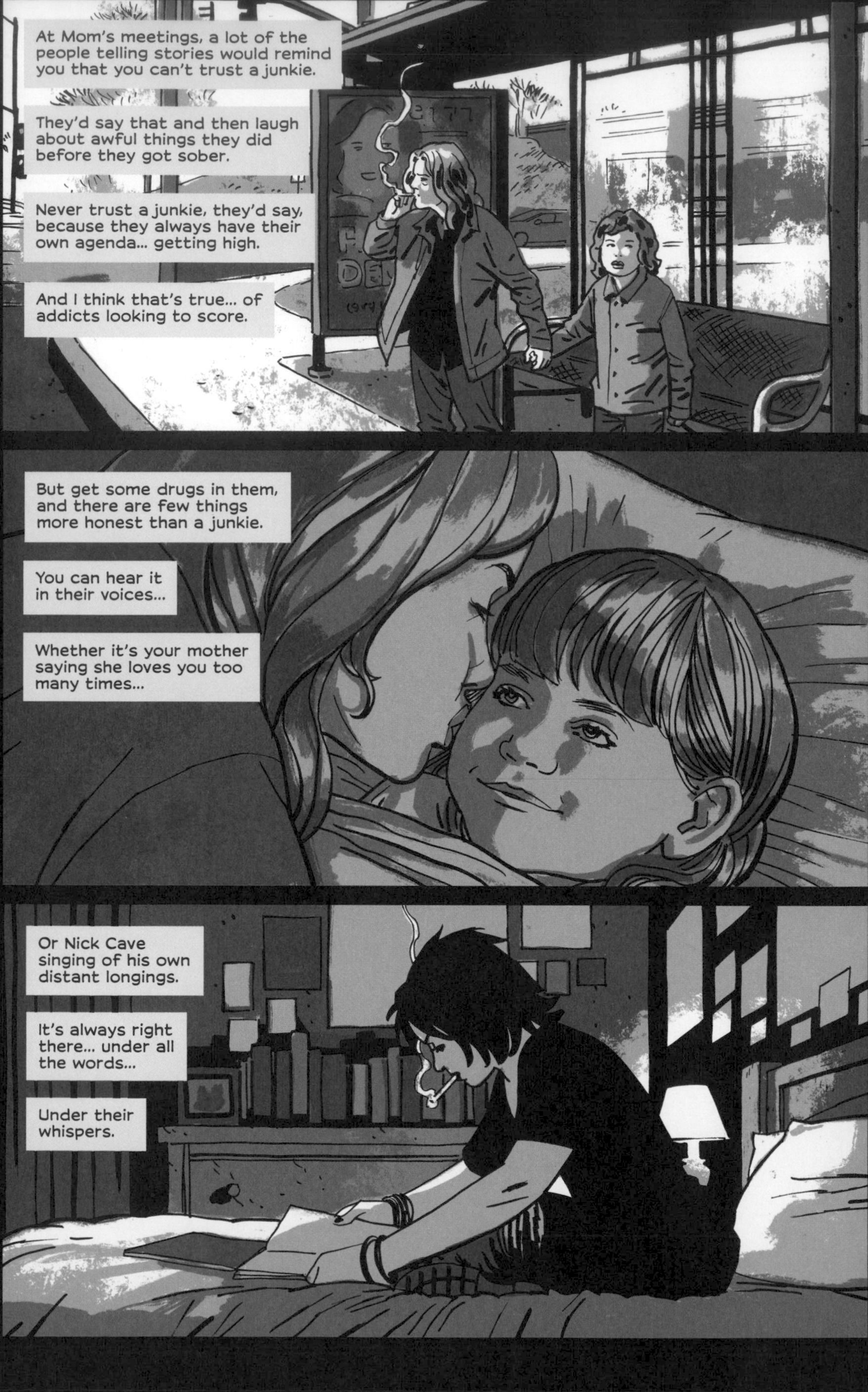
At Mom's meetings, a lot of the people telling stories would remind you that you can't trust a junkie.
They'd say that and then laugh about awful things they did before they got sober.
Never trust a junkie, they'd say, because they always have their own agenda... getting high.
And I think that's true... of addicts looking to score.
But get some drugs in them, and there are few things more honest than a junkie.
You can hear it in their voices...
Whether it's your mother saying she loves you too many times...
Or Nick Cave singing of his own distant longings.
It's always right there... under all the words...
Under their whispers.

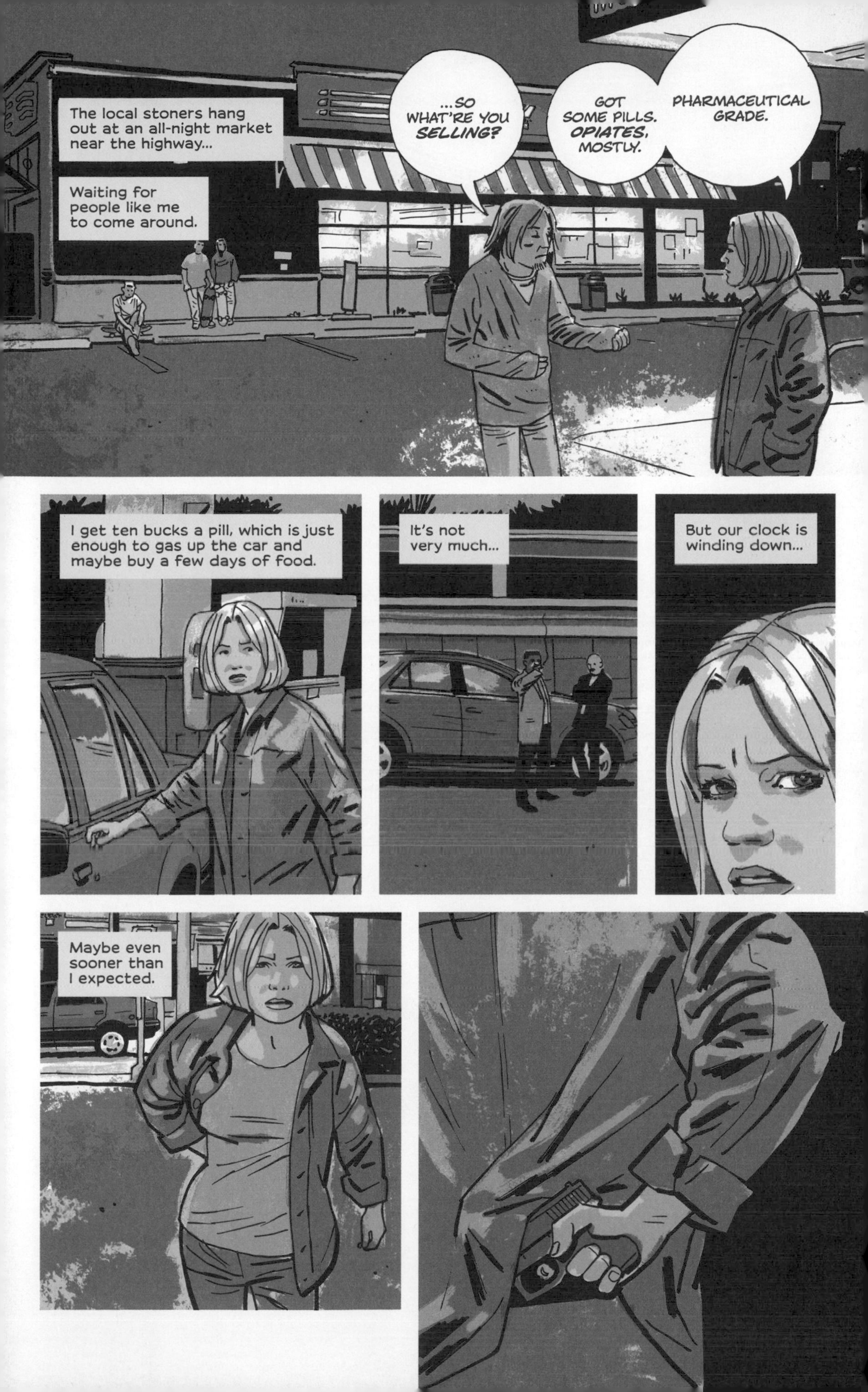

The local stoners hang out at an all-night market near the highway...
Waiting for people like me to come around.
...SO WHAT'RE YOU SELLING?
GOT SOME PILLS. OPIATES, MOSTLY.
PHARMACEUTICAL GRADE.
I get ten bucks a pill, which is just enough to gas up the car and maybe buy a few days of food.
It's not very much...
But our clock is winding down...
Maybe even sooner than I expected.

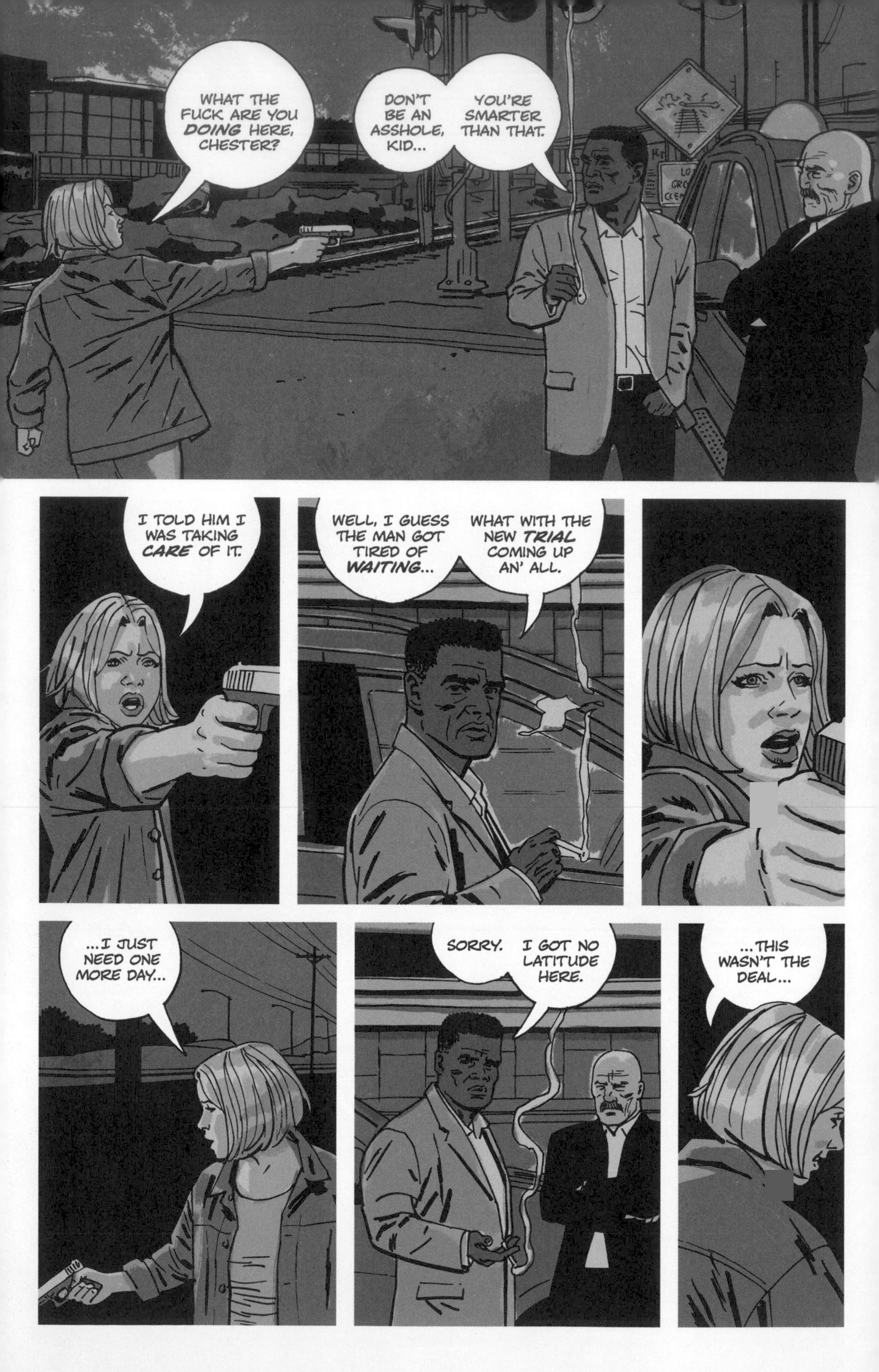
WHAT THE FUCK ARE YOU *DOING* HERE, CHESTER?
DON'T BE AN ASSHOLE, KID...
YOU'RE SMARTER THAN THAT.
I TOLD HIM I WAS TAKING *CARE* OF IT.
WELL, I GUESS THE MAN GOT TIRED OF *WAITING*...
WHAT WITH THE NEW *TRIAL* COMING UP AN' ALL.
...I JUST NEED ONE MORE DAY...
SORRY.
I GOT NO LATITUDE HERE.
...THIS WASN'T THE DEAL...

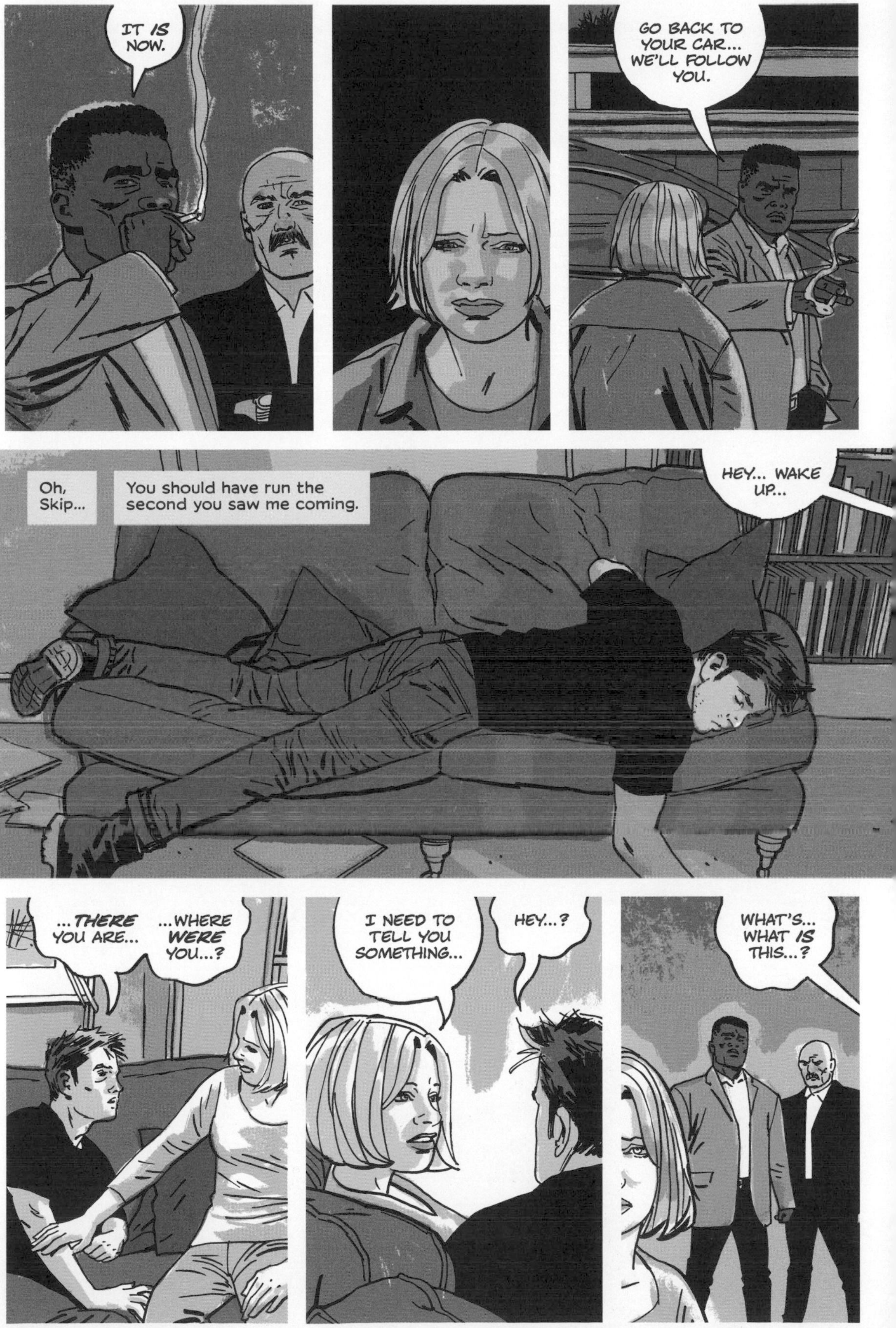
IT *IS* NOW.
GO BACK TO YOUR CAR... WE'LL FOLLOW YOU.
Oh, Skip...
You should have run the second you saw me coming.
HEY... WAKE UP...
...*THERE* YOU ARE...
...WHERE *WERE* YOU...?
I NEED TO TELL YOU SOMETHING...
HEY...?
WHAT'S... WHAT *IS* THIS...?

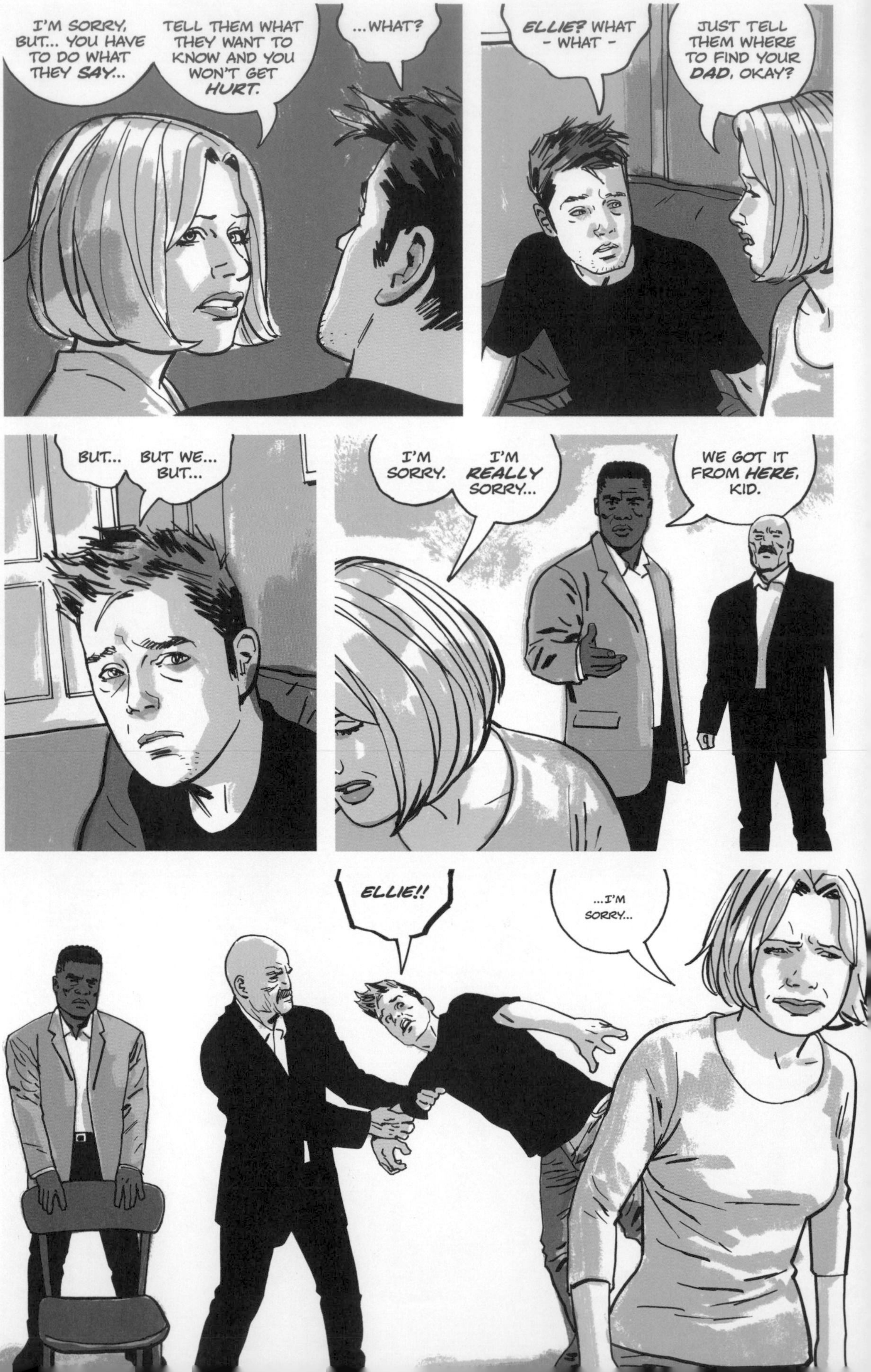
I'M SORRY, BUT... YOU HAVE TO DO WHAT THEY SAY...
TELL THEM WHAT THEY WANT TO KNOW AND YOU WON'T GET HURT.
...WHAT?
ELLIE? WHAT - WHAT -
JUST TELL THEM WHERE TO FIND YOUR DAD, OKAY?
BUT... BUT WE... BUT...
I'M SORRY.
I'M REALLY SORRY...
WE GOT IT FROM HERE, KID.
ELLIE!!
...I'M SORRY...

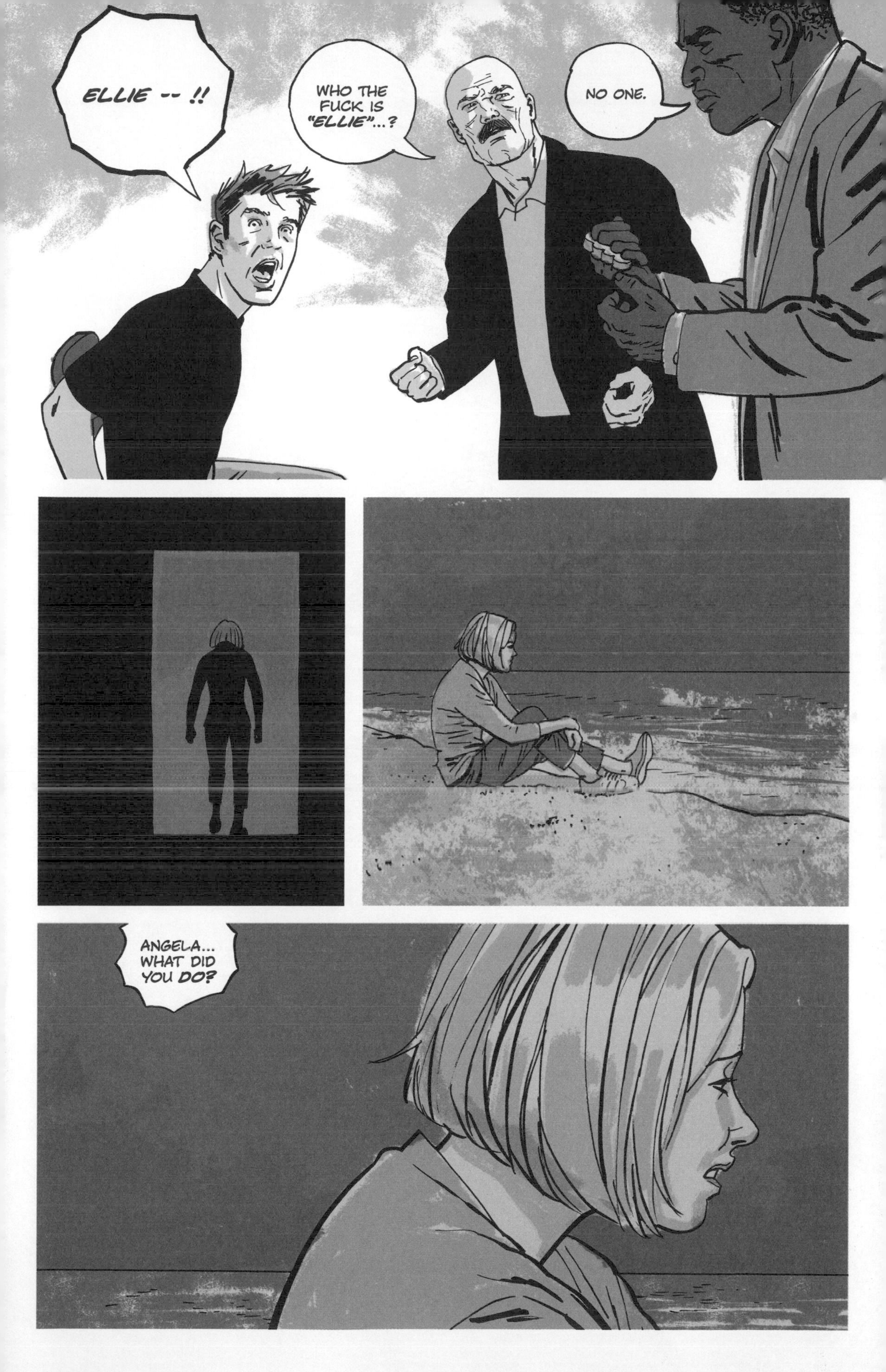
ELLIE -- !!
WHO THE FUCK IS "ELLIE"...?
NO ONE.
ANGELA... WHAT DID YOU DO?

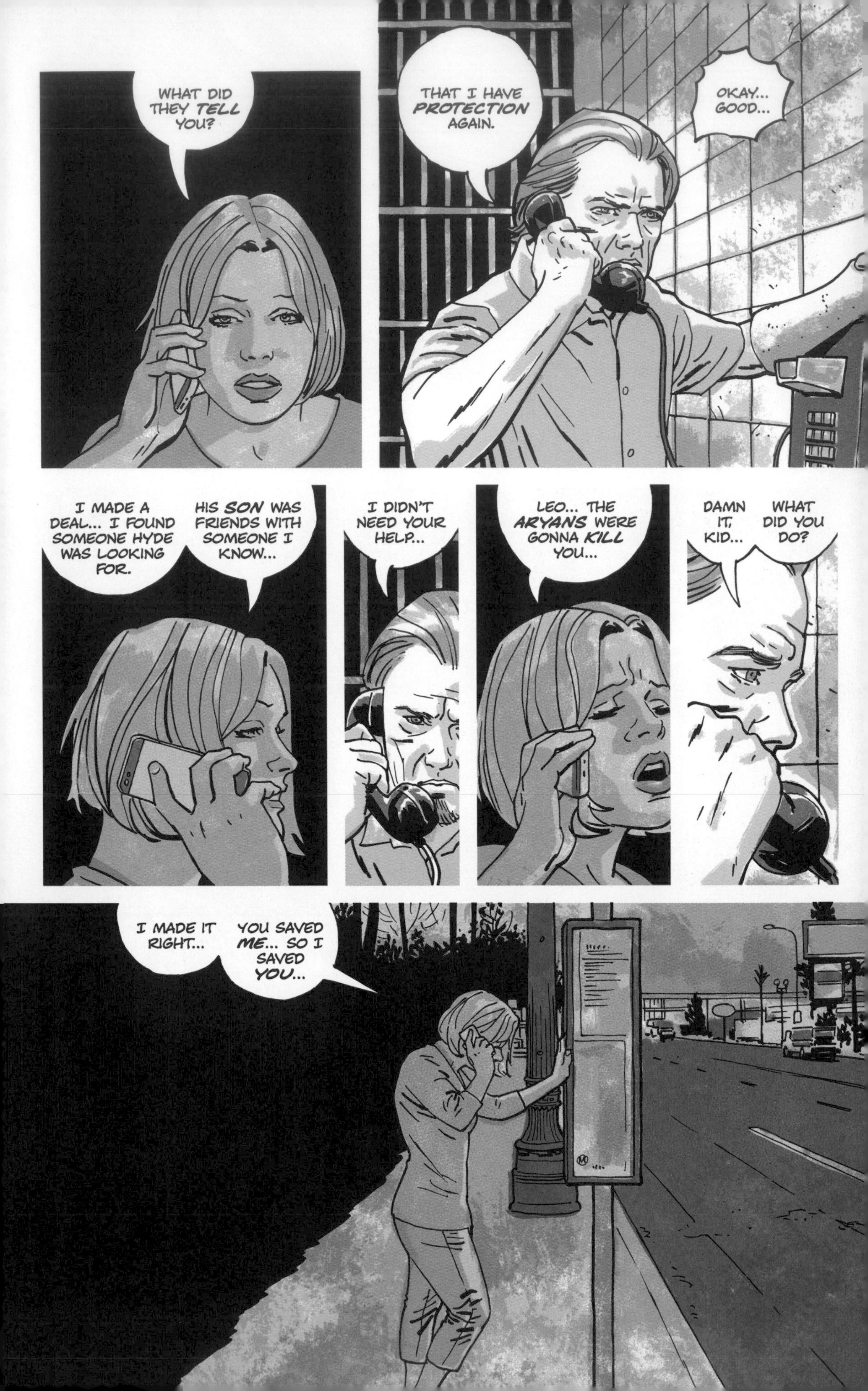

WHAT DID THEY TELL YOU?
THAT I HAVE PROTECTION AGAIN.
OKAY... GOOD...
I MADE A DEAL... I FOUND SOMEONE HYDE WAS LOOKING FOR.
HIS SON WAS FRIENDS WITH SOMEONE I KNOW...
I DIDN'T NEED YOUR HELP...
LEO... THE ARYANS WERE GONNA KILL YOU...
DAMN IT, KID...
WHAT DID YOU DO?
I MADE IT RIGHT...
YOU SAVED ME... SO I SAVED YOU...

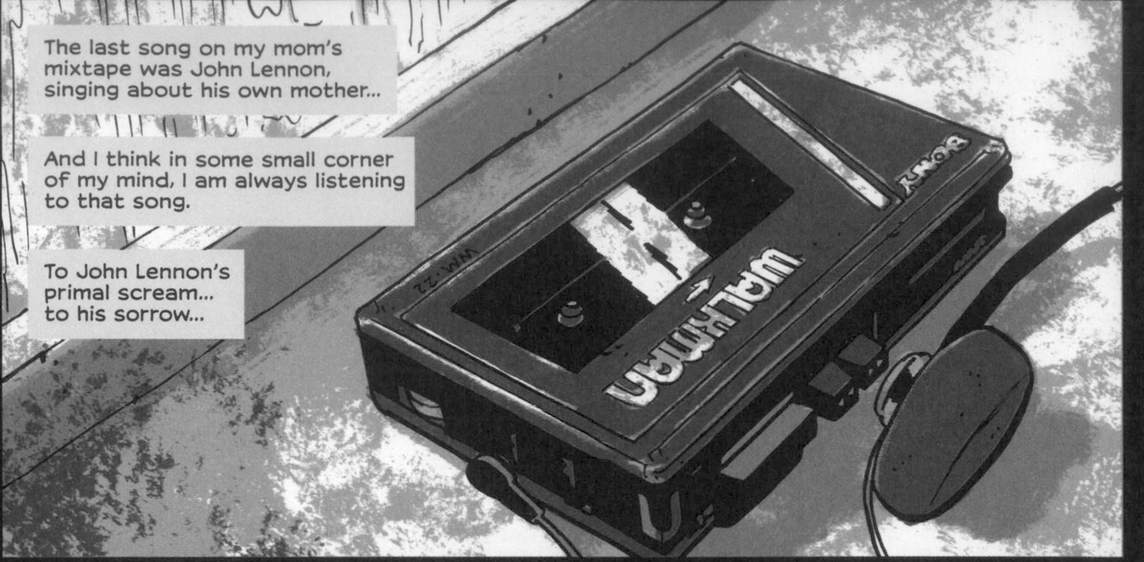
The last song on my mom's mixtape was John Lennon, singing about his own mother...
And I think in some small corner of my mind, I am always listening to that song.
To John Lennon's primal scream... to his sorrow...
WALKMAN
WM-22
SONY

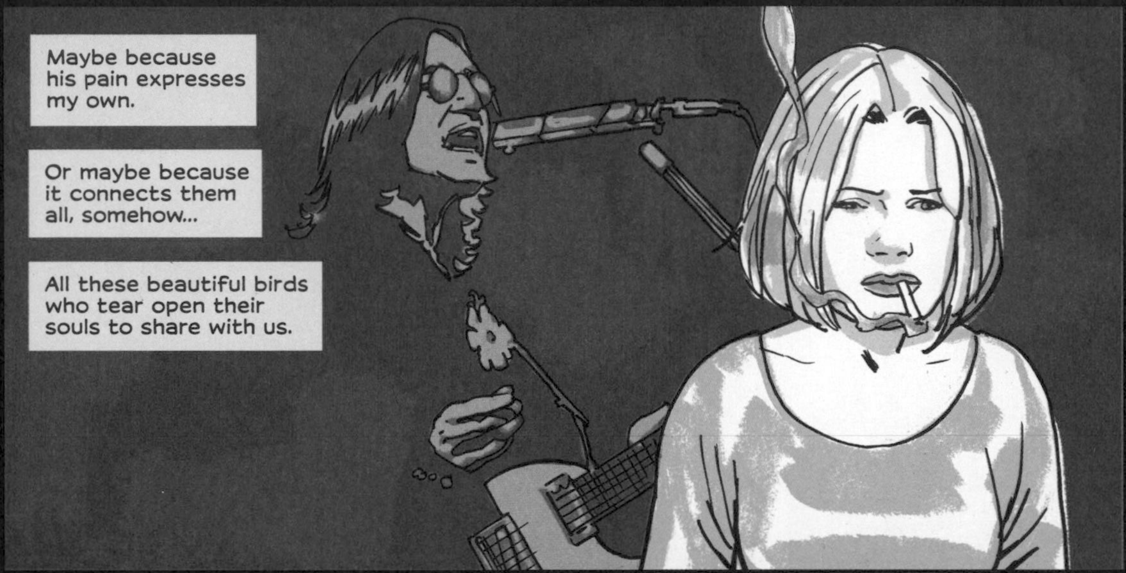
Maybe because his pain expresses my own.
Or maybe because it connects them all, somehow...
All these beautiful birds who tear open their souls to share with us.

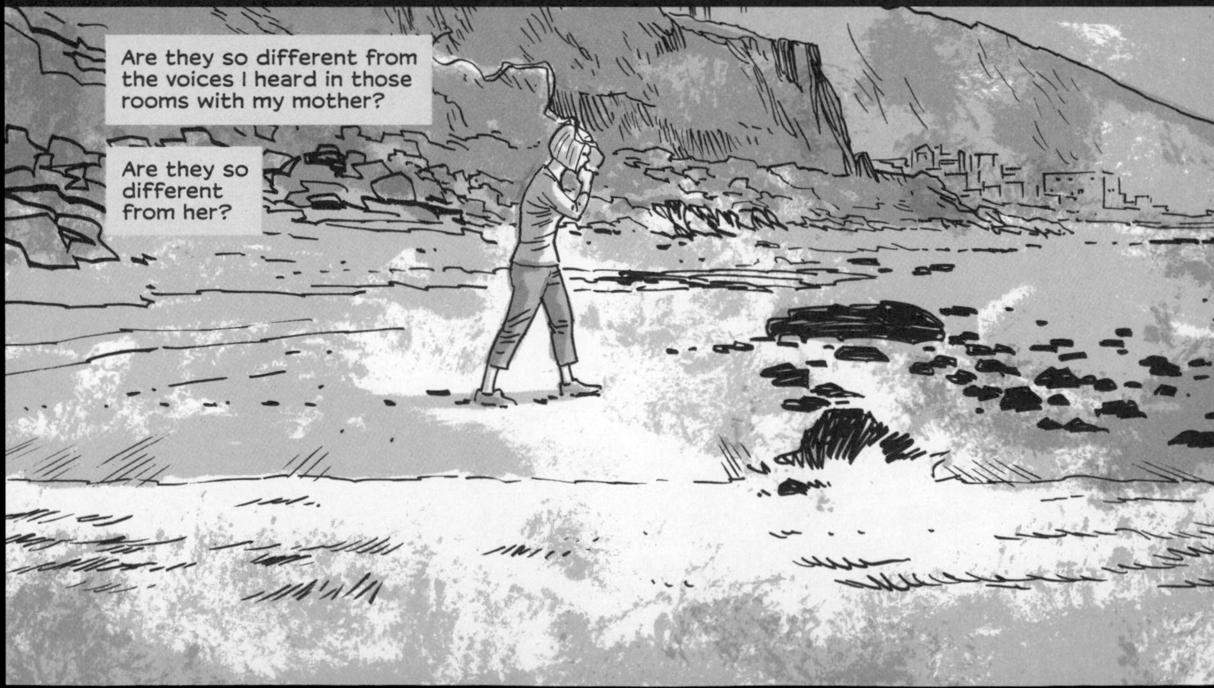
Are they so different from the voices I heard in those rooms with my mother?
Are they so different from her?

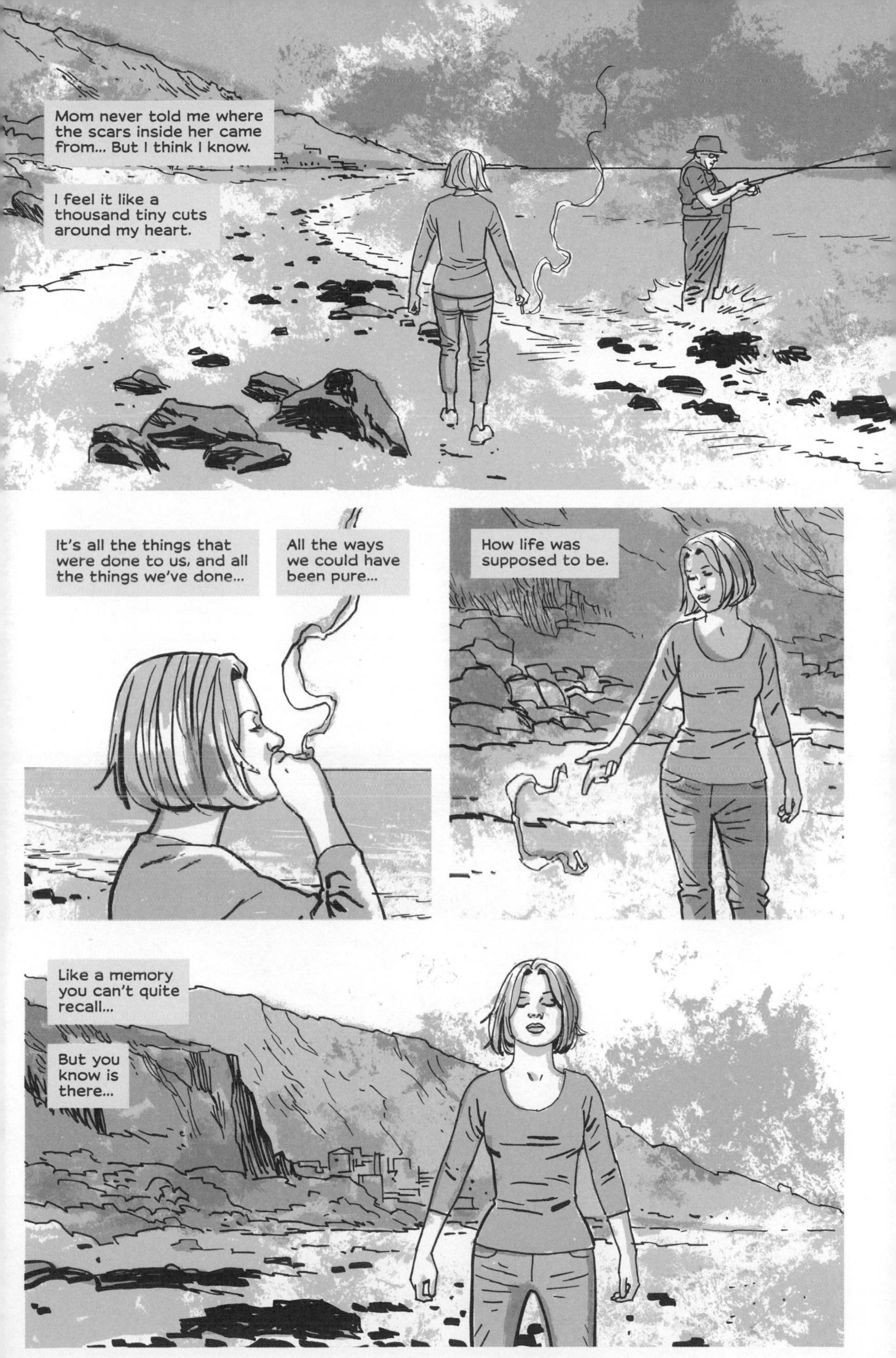
Mom never told me where the scars inside her came from... But I think I know.
I feel it like a thousand tiny cuts around my heart.
It's all the things that were done to us, and all the things we've done...
All the ways we could have been pure...
How life was supposed to be.
Like a memory you can't quite recall...
But you know is there...

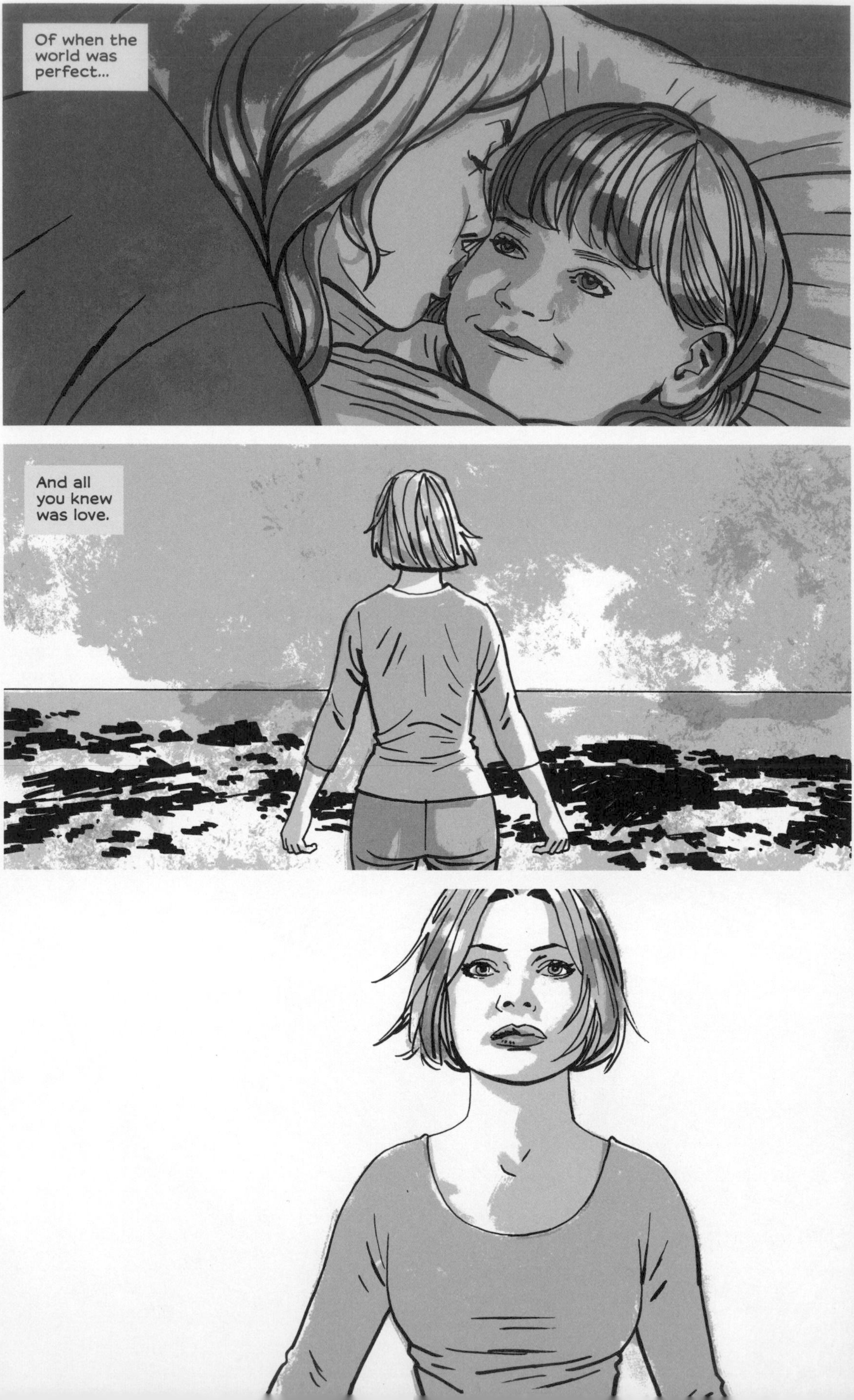
Of when the world was perfect...
And all you knew was love.

OTHER BOOKS BY BRUBAKER AND PHILLIPS:

CRIMINAL: Coward   ISBN: 978-1-63215-170-4

CRIMINAL: Lawless   ISBN: 978-1-63215-203-9

CRIMINAL: The Dead And The Dying   ISBN: 978-1-63215-233-6

CRIMINAL: Bad Night   ISBN: 978-1-63215-260-2

CRIMINAL: The Sinners   ISBN: 978-1-63215-298-5

CRIMINAL: The Last Of The Innocent   ISBN: 978-1-63215-299-2

CRIMINAL: Wrong Time, Wrong Place   ISBN: 978-1-63215-877-2

CRIMINAL The Deluxe Edition Volume One   ISBN: 978-1-5343-0541-0

CRIMINAL The Deluxe Edition Volume Two   ISBN: 978-1-5343-0543-4

FATALE The Deluxe Edition Volume One   ISBN: 978-1-60706-942-3

FATALE The Deluxe Edition Volume Two   ISBN: 978-1-63215-503-0

FATALE Book One: Death Chases Me   ISBN: 978-1-60706-563-0

FATALE Book Two: The Devil's Business   ISBN: 978-1-60706-618-7

FATALE Book Three: West Of Hell   ISBN: 978-1-60706-743-6

FATALE Book Four: Pray For Rain   ISBN: 978-1-60706-835-8

FATALE Book Five: Curse The Demon   ISBN: 978-1-63215-007-3

THE FADE OUT   ISBN: 978-1-5343-0860-2

THE FADE OUT Deluxe Edition   ISBN: 978-1-63215-911-3

KILL OR BE KILLED Volume One   ISBN: 978-1-5343-0028-6

KILL OR BE KILLED Volume Two   ISBN: 978-1-5343-0228-0

KILL OR BE KILLED Volume Three   ISBN: 978-1-5343-0471-0

KILL OR BE KILLED Volume Four   ISBN: 978-1-5343-0651-6

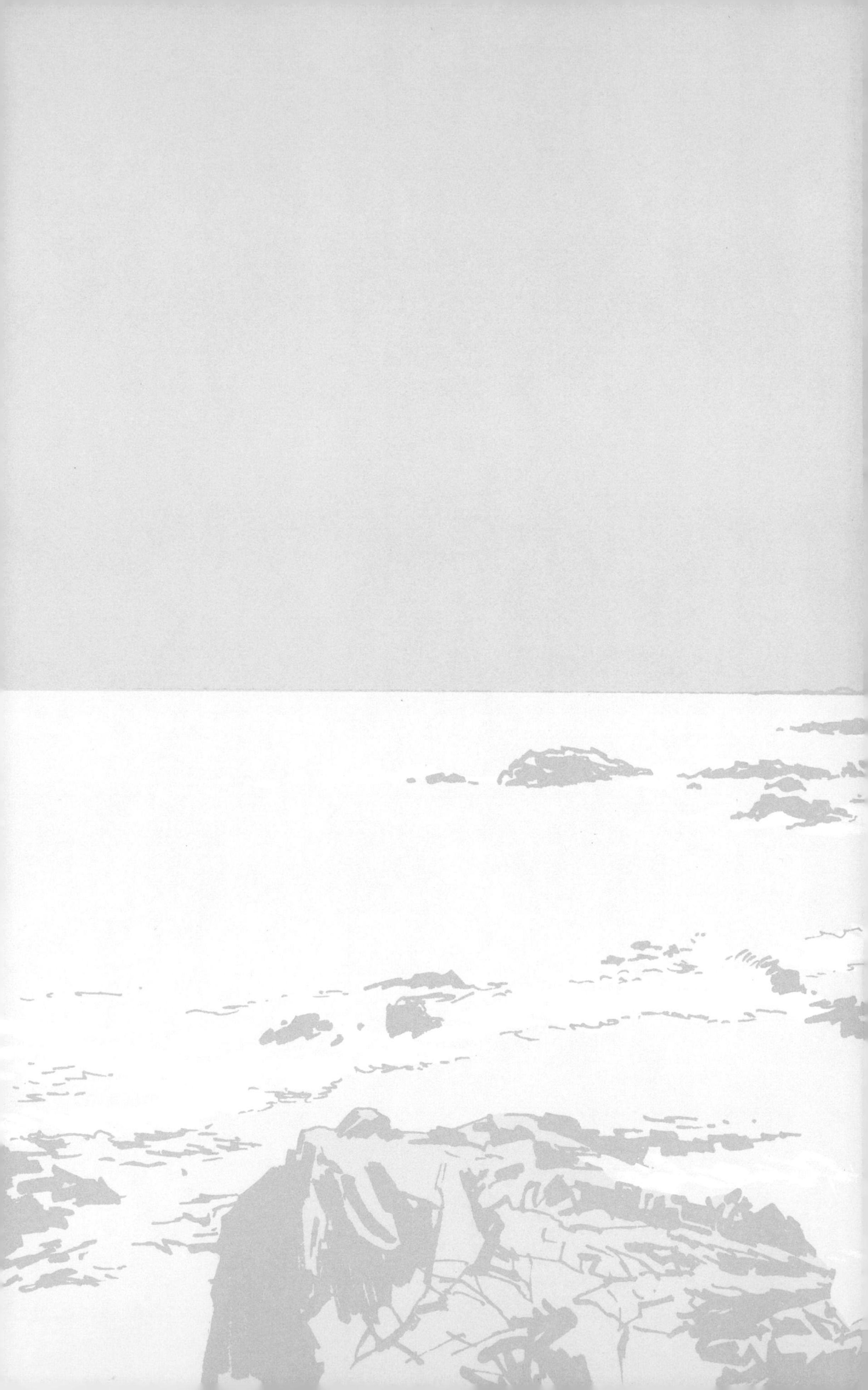